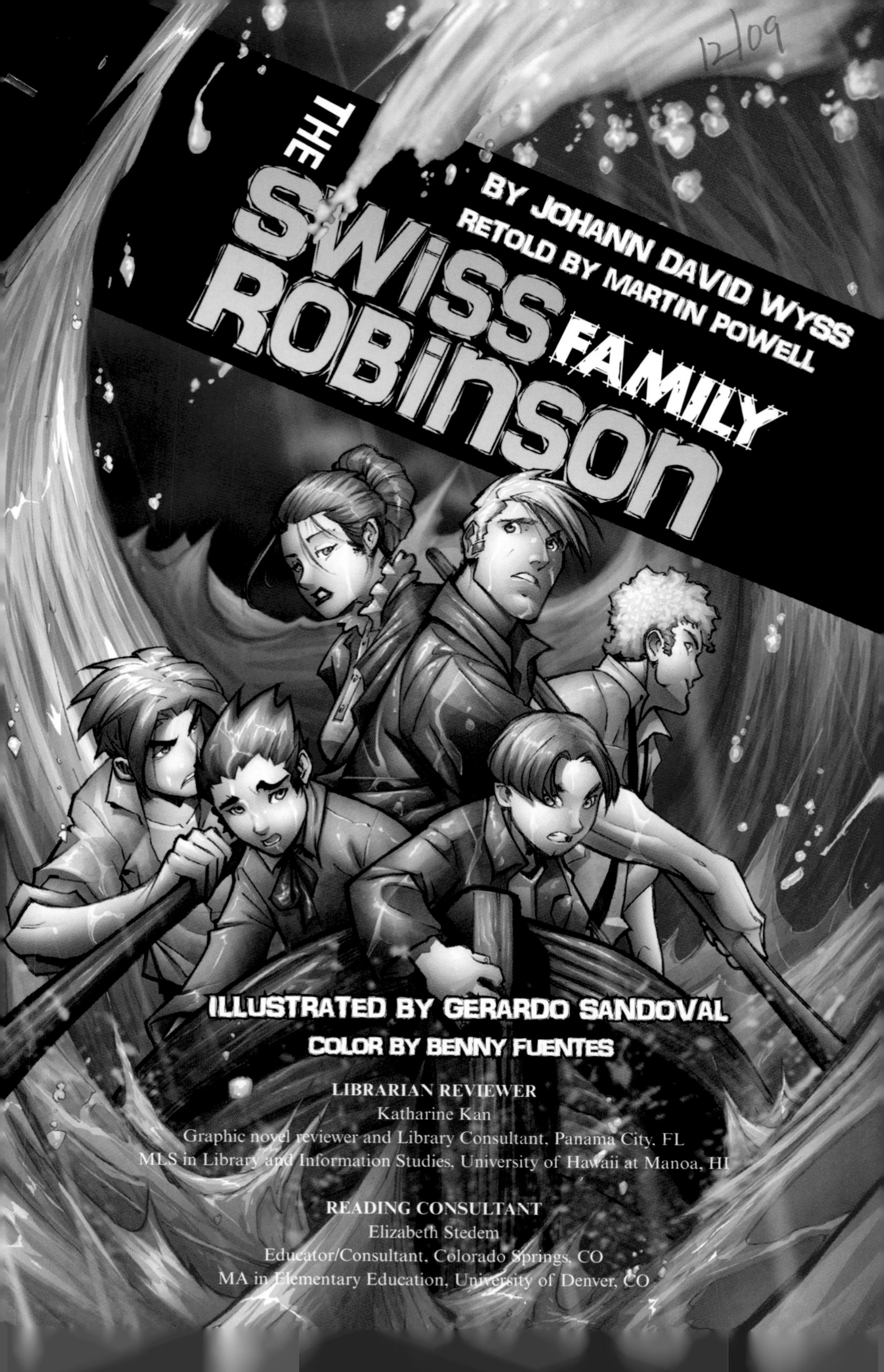

The Swiss Family Robinson

By Johann David Wyss

Retold by Martin Powell

Illustrated by Gerardo Sandoval

Color by Benny Fuentes

LIBRARIAN REVIEWER
Katharine Kan
Graphic novel reviewer and Library Consultant, Panama City, FL
MLS in Library and Information Studies, University of Hawaii at Manoa, HI

READING CONSULTANT
Elizabeth Stedem
Educator/Consultant, Colorado Springs, CO
MA in Elementary Education, University of Denver, CO

Graphic Revolve is published by Stone Arch Books
151 Good Counsel Drive, P.O. Box 669
Mankato, Minnesota 56002
www.stonearchbooks.com

Copyright © 2009 by Stone Arch Books

Library of Congress Cataloging-in-Publication Data
Powell, Martin.
    The Swiss Family Robinson / by Johann David Wyss; retold by Martin Powell;
illustrated by Gerardo Sandoval.
    p. cm. — (Graphic Revolve)
    ISBN 978-1-4342-0756-2 (library binding)
    ISBN 978-1-4342-0852-1 (pbk.)
    1. Graphic novels. [1. Graphic novels. 2. Survival—Fiction. 3. Family life—Fiction.
4. Islands—Fiction.] I. Sandoval, Gerardo, 1974– ill. II. Wyss, Johann David, 1743–1818.
Schweizerische Robinson. III. Title.
PZ7.7.P69Swi 2009
[Fic]—dc22   2008006249

Summary: A family from Switzerland is shipwrecked on a deserted island. They discover
that the island is filled with plants and animals they've never seen before. Unfortunately,
not all of the creatures are friendly.

Art Director: Heather Kindseth
Graphic Designer: Kay Fraser

1 2 3 4 5 6 13 12 11 10 09 08

Printed in the United States of America

TABLE OF CONTENTS

INTRODUCING (Cast of Characters) 4

CHAPTER 1
Shipwrecked! 6

CHAPTER 2
Building a New Home. 22

CHAPTER 3
A Deadly Mystery 34

CHAPTER 4
Island of Good Fortune. 42

CHAPTER 5
Fritz's Discovery. 47

CHAPTER 6
The Cave Creature 53

CHAPTER 7
Rescued from Paradise 59

INTRODUCING . . .

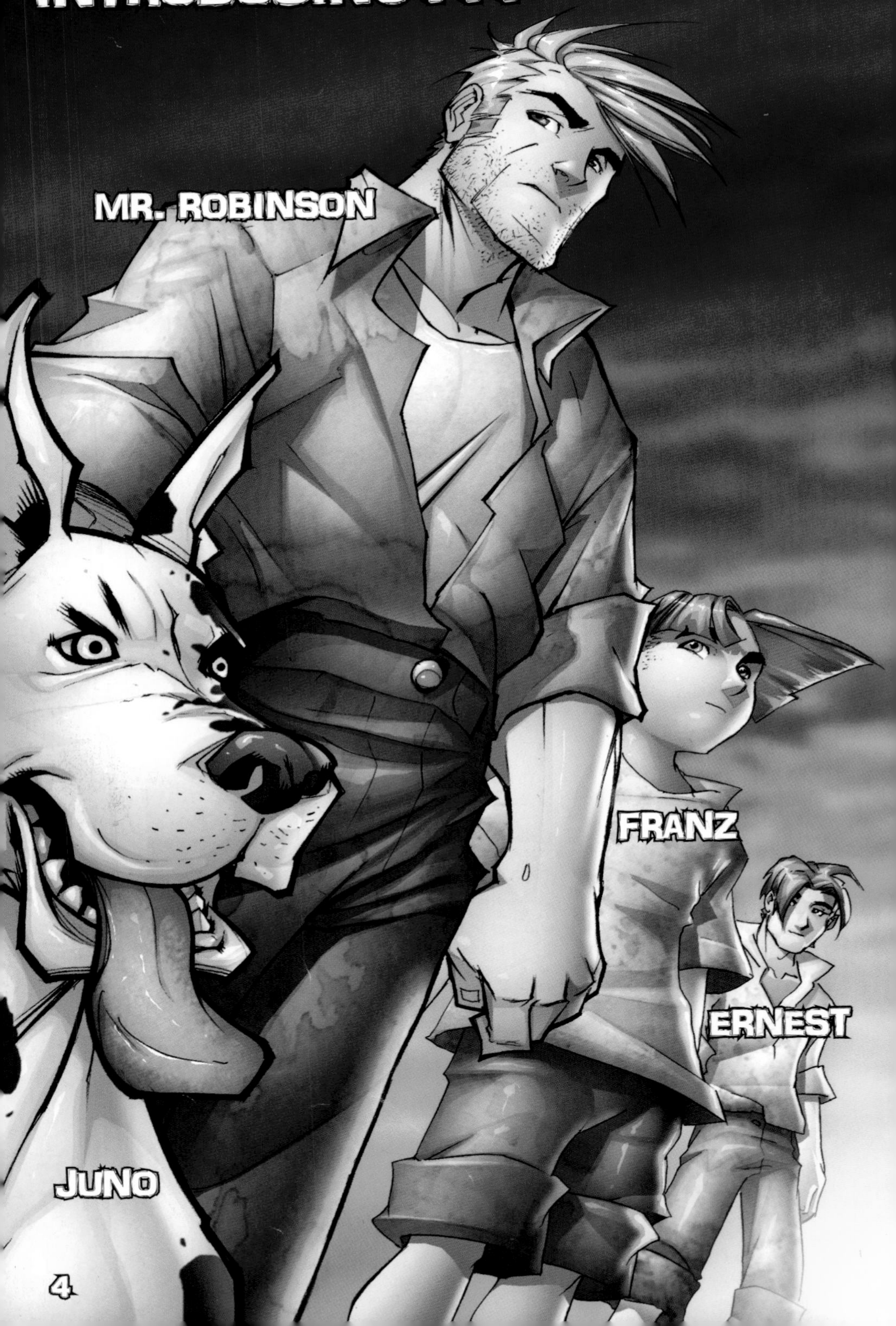
MR. ROBINSON
FRANZ
ERNEST
JUNO

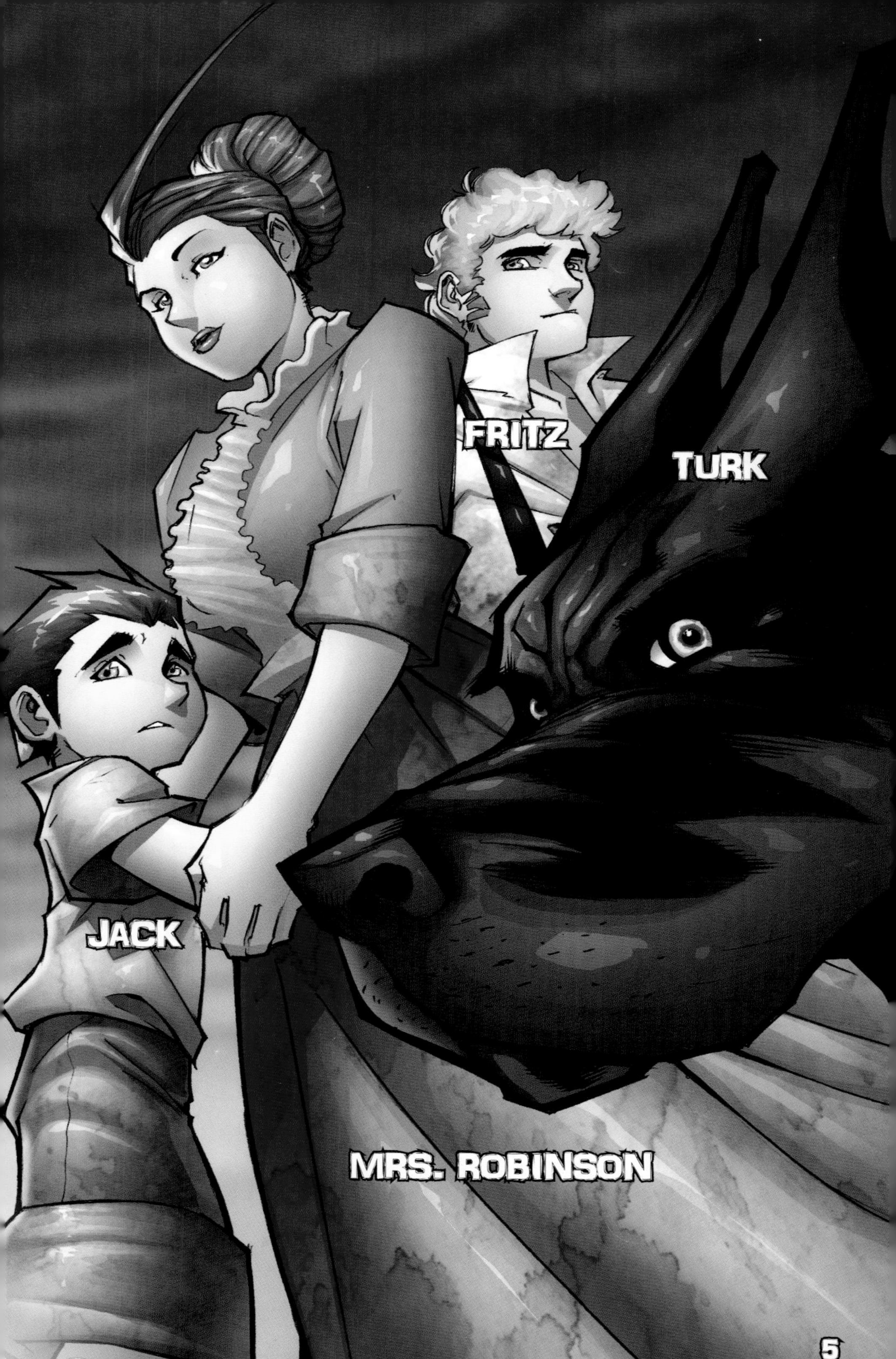
FRITZ
TURK
JACK
MRS. ROBINSON

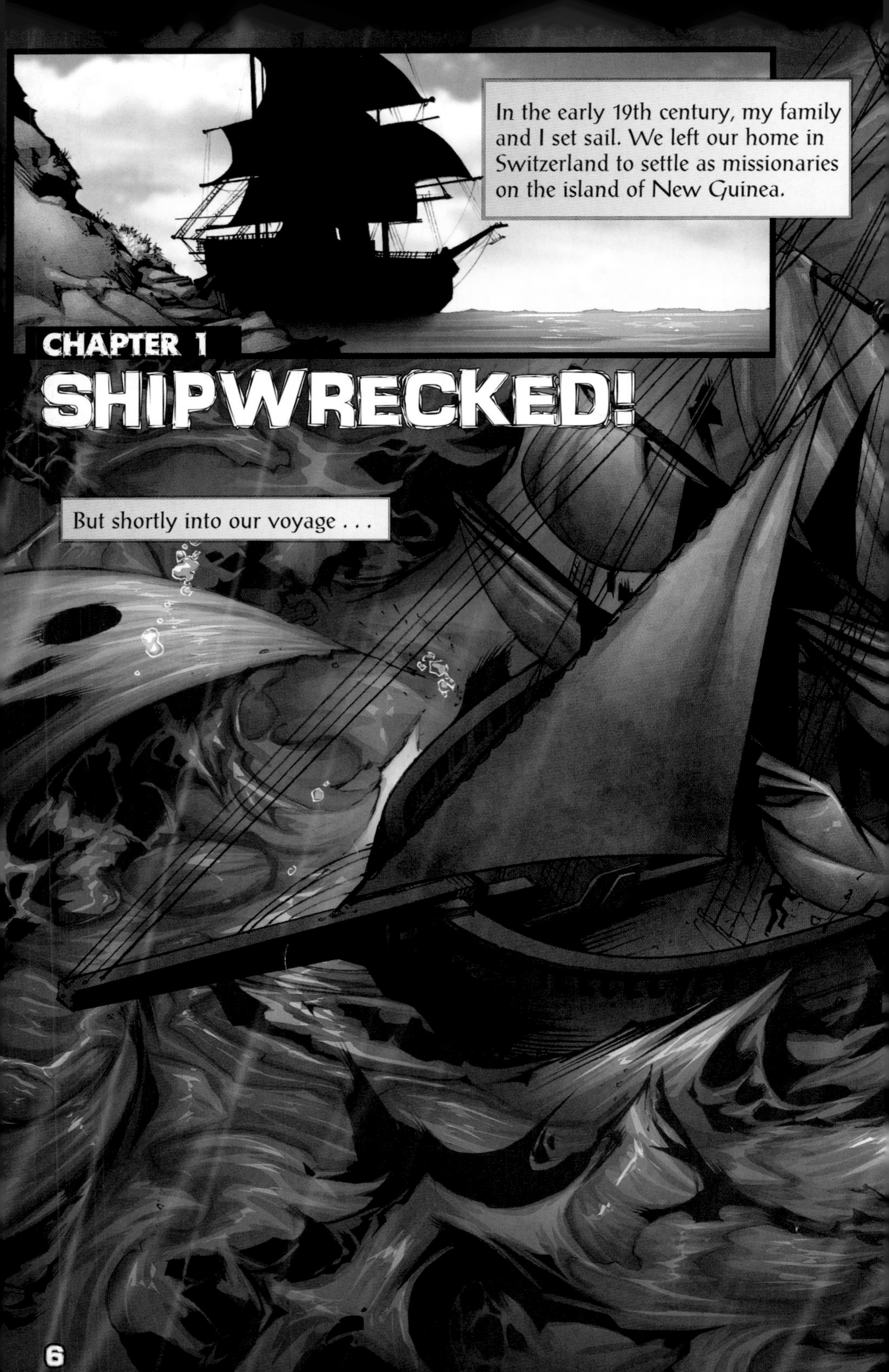
In the early 19th century, my family and I set sail. We left our home in Switzerland to settle as missionaries on the island of New Guinea.
CHAPTER 1
SHIPWRECKED!
But shortly into our voyage . . .

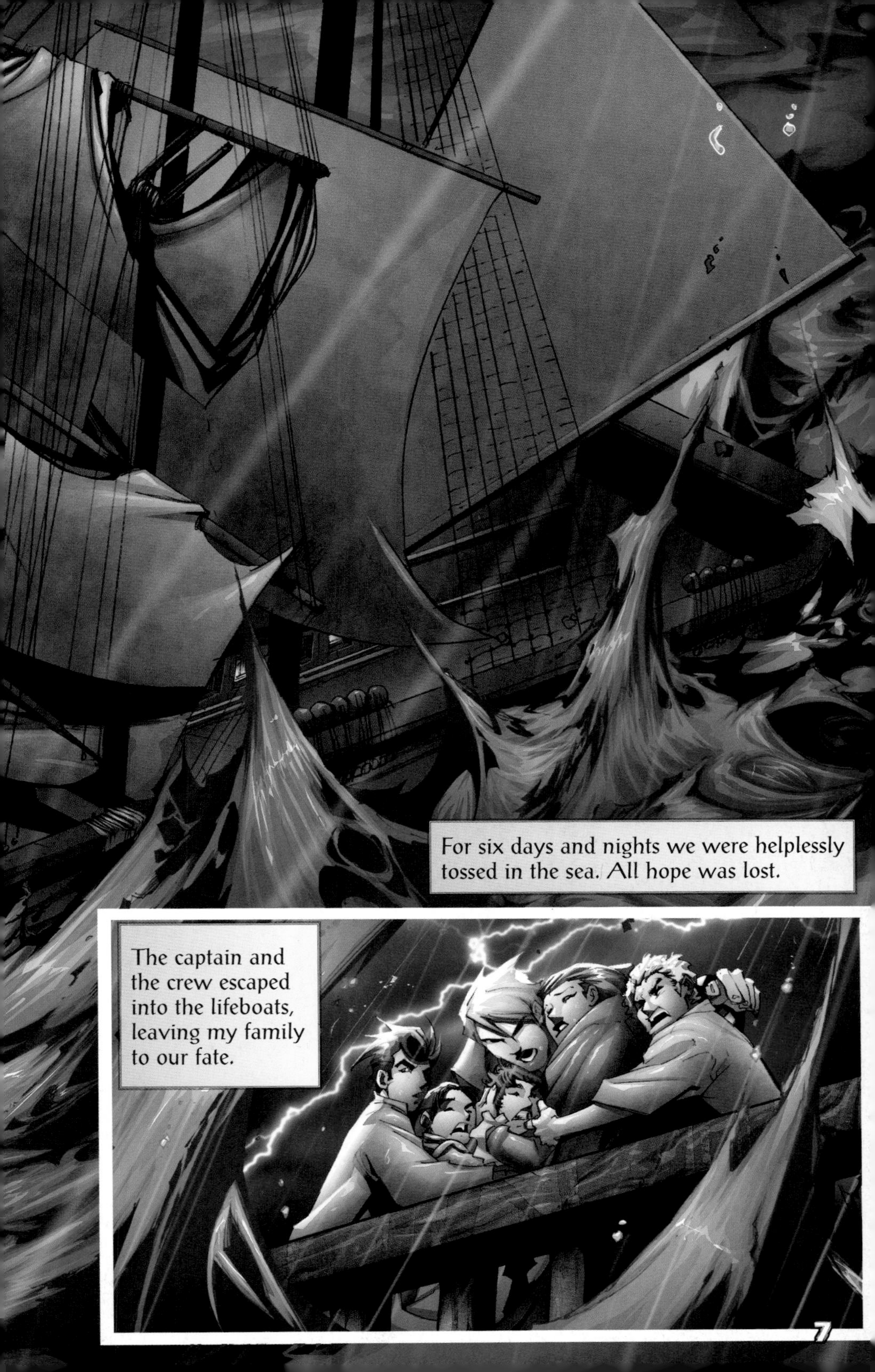
For six days and nights we were helplessly tossed in the sea. All hope was lost.
The captain and the crew escaped into the lifeboats, leaving my family to our fate.

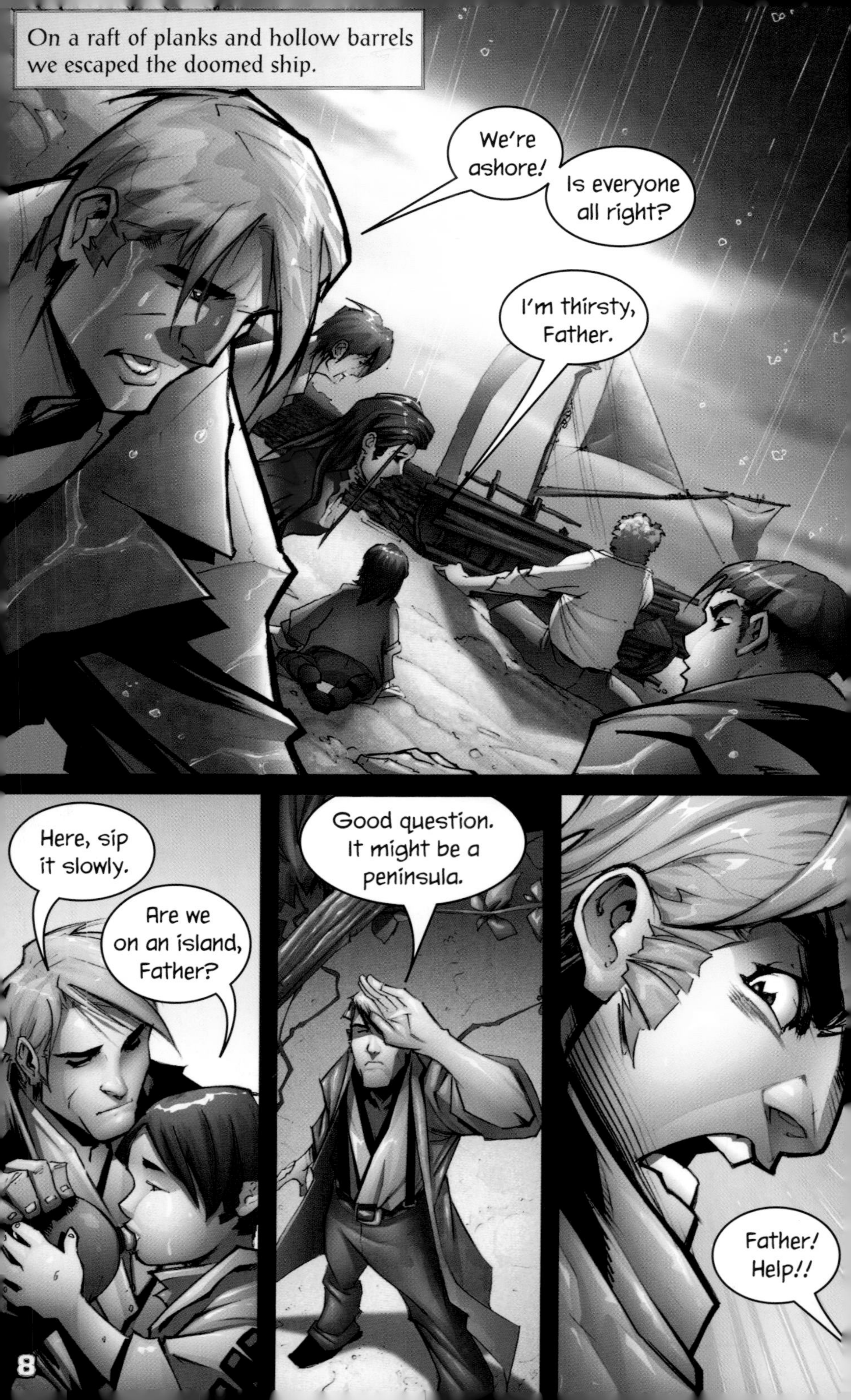
On a raft of planks and hollow barrels we escaped the doomed ship.
We're ashore!
Is everyone all right?
I'm thirsty, Father.
Here, sip it slowly.
Are we on an island, Father?
Good question. It might be a peninsula.
Father! Help!!

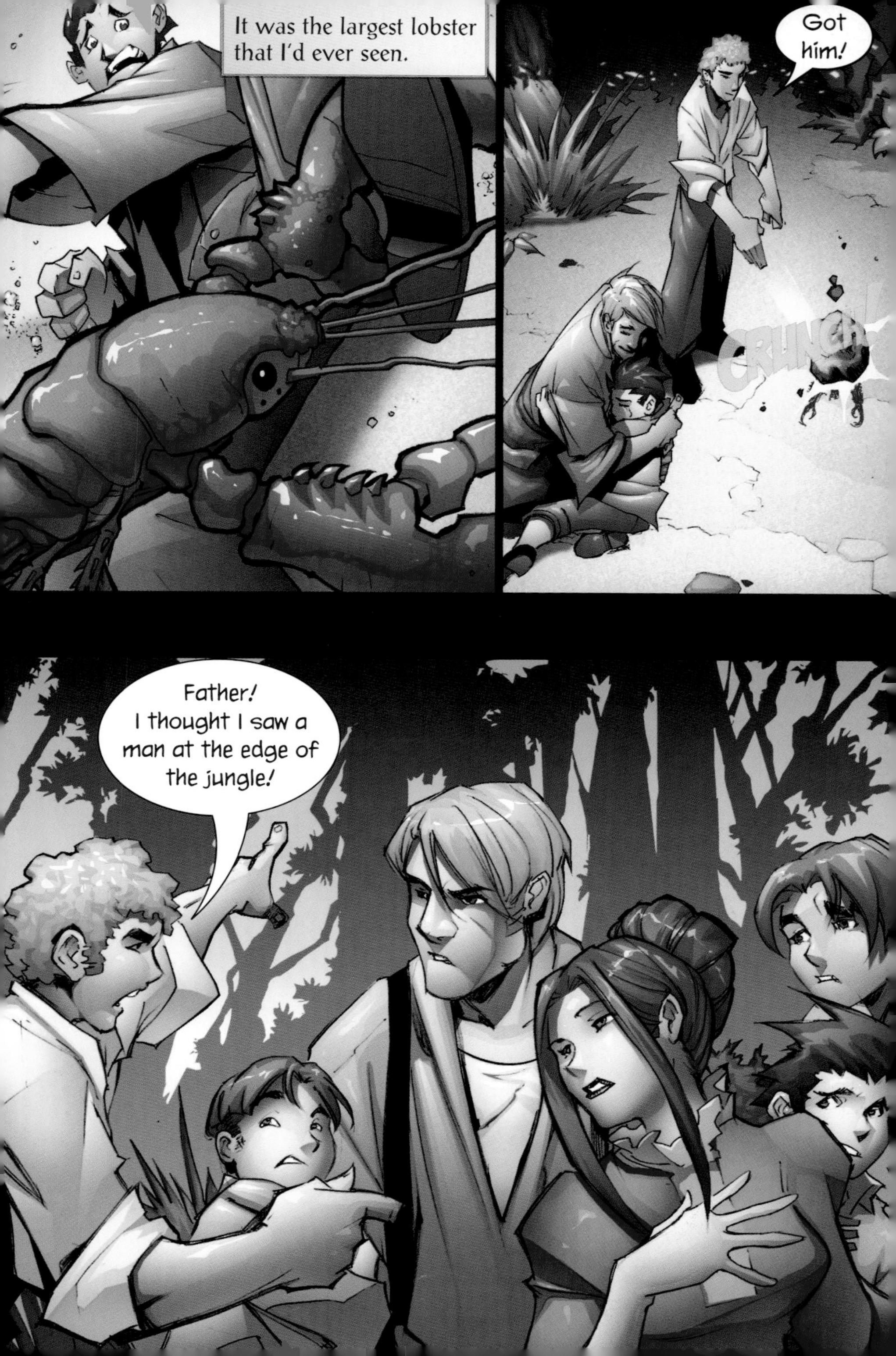
It was the largest lobster that I'd ever seen.
Got him!
CRUNCH
Father! I thought I saw a man at the edge of the jungle!

There might be natives here.
Jack, you stay with Franz and your mother. We won't be gone long.
The woods are so wild!
Keep your voice low, Fritz. We need to be aware of every shadow from now on.

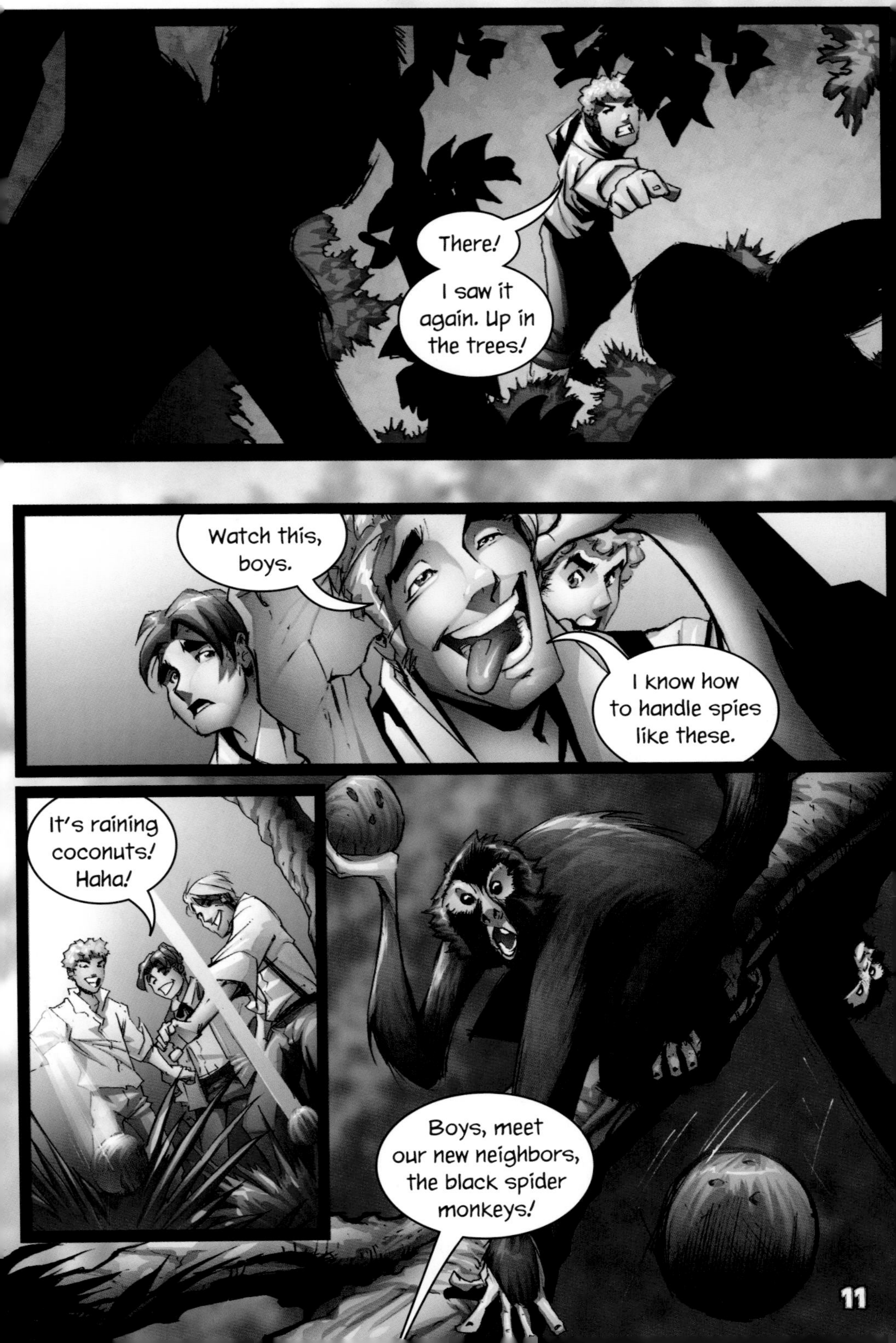
There!
I saw it again. Up in the trees!
Watch this, boys.
I know how to handle spies like these.
It's raining coconuts! Haha!
Boys, meet our new neighbors, the black spider monkeys!

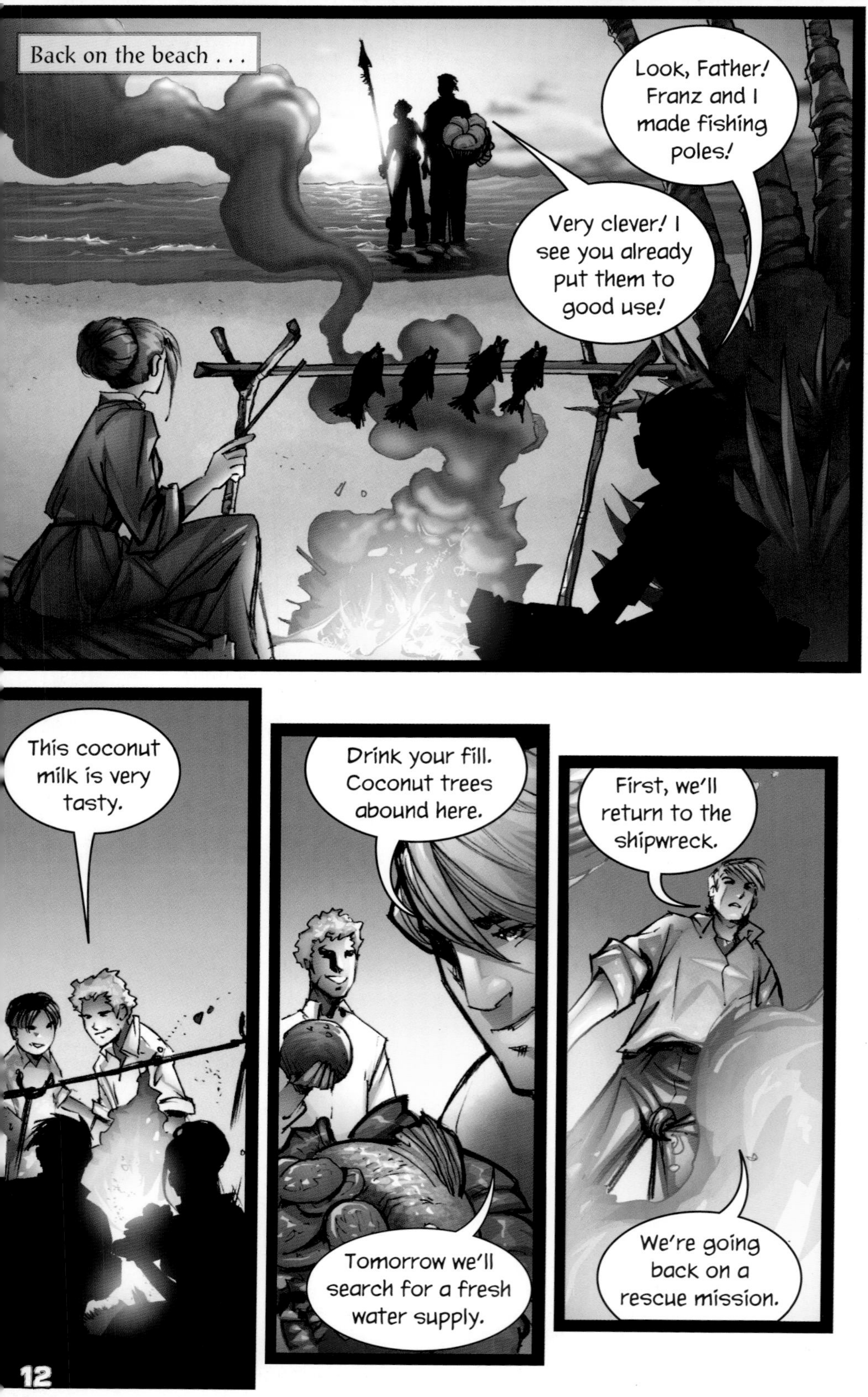
Back on the beach . . .
Look, Father! Franz and I made fishing poles!
Very clever! I see you already put them to good use!
This coconut milk is very tasty.
Drink your fill. Coconut trees abound here.
Tomorrow we'll search for a fresh water supply.
First, we'll return to the shipwreck.
We're going back on a rescue mission.

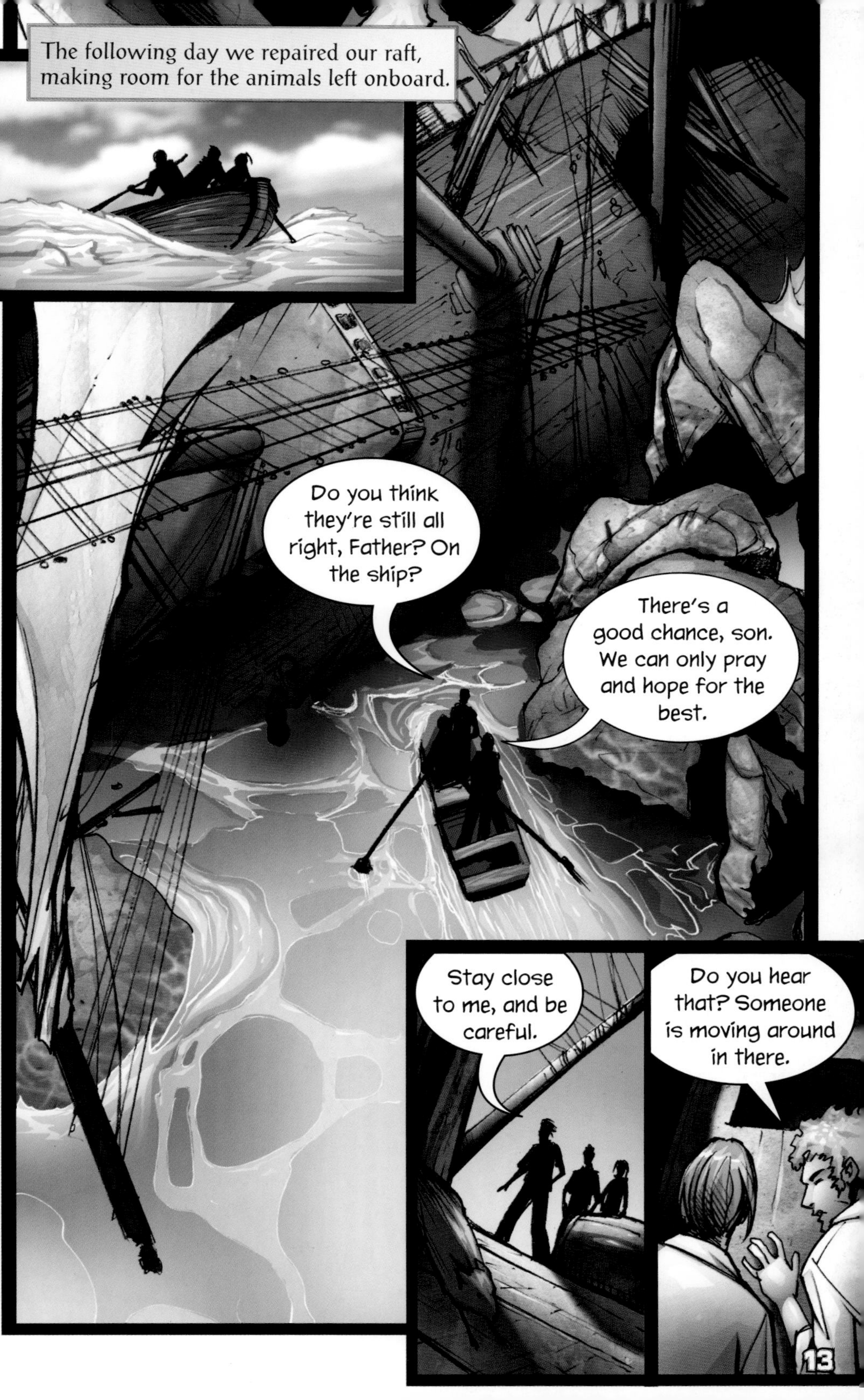
The following day we repaired our raft, making room for the animals left onboard.
Do you think they're still all right, Father? On the ship?
There's a good chance, son. We can only pray and hope for the best.
Stay close to me, and be careful.
Do you hear that? Someone is moving around in there.

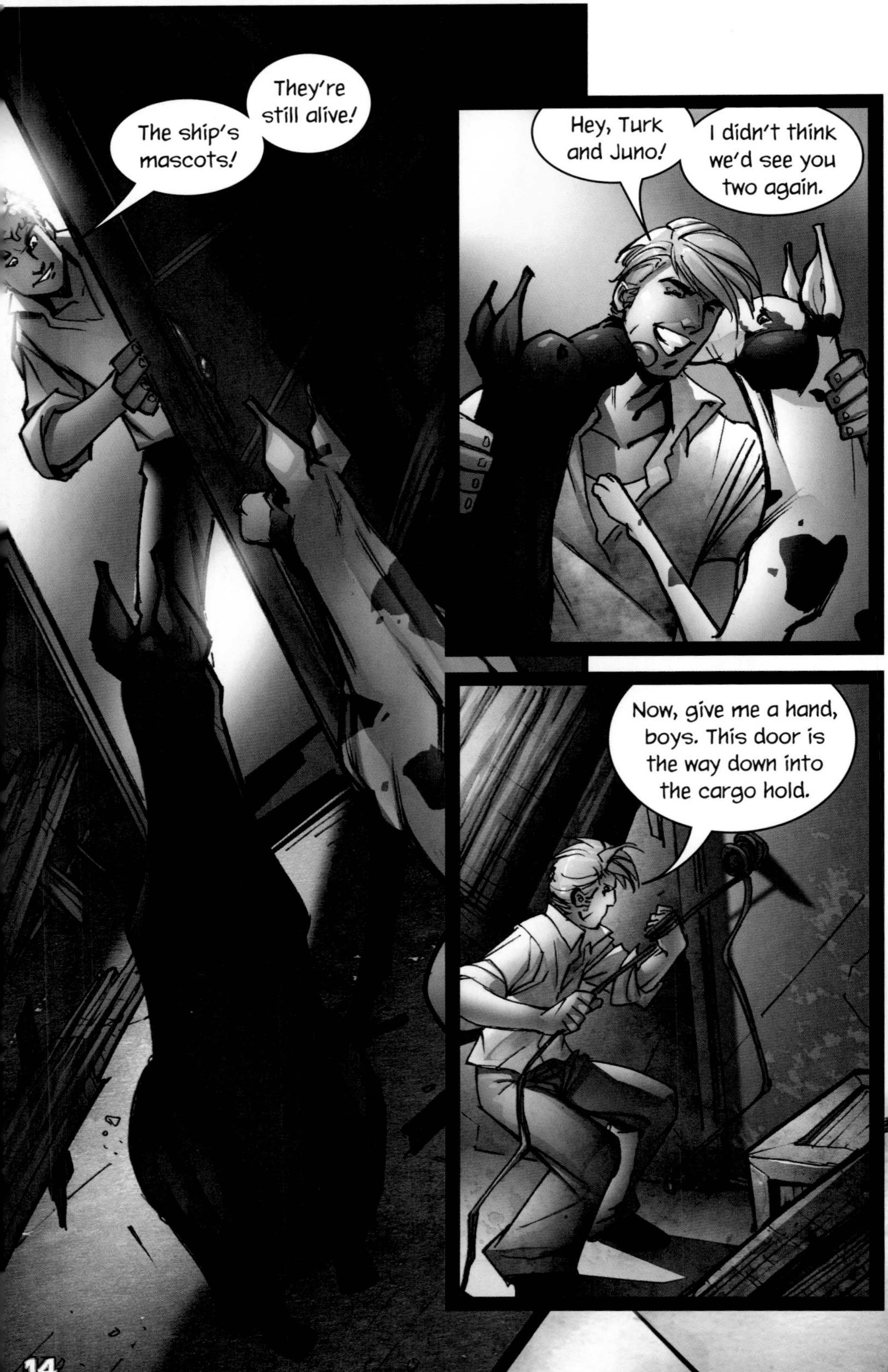
They're still alive!
The ship's mascots!
Hey, Turk and Juno!
I didn't think we'd see you two again.
Now, give me a hand, boys. This door is the way down into the cargo hold.

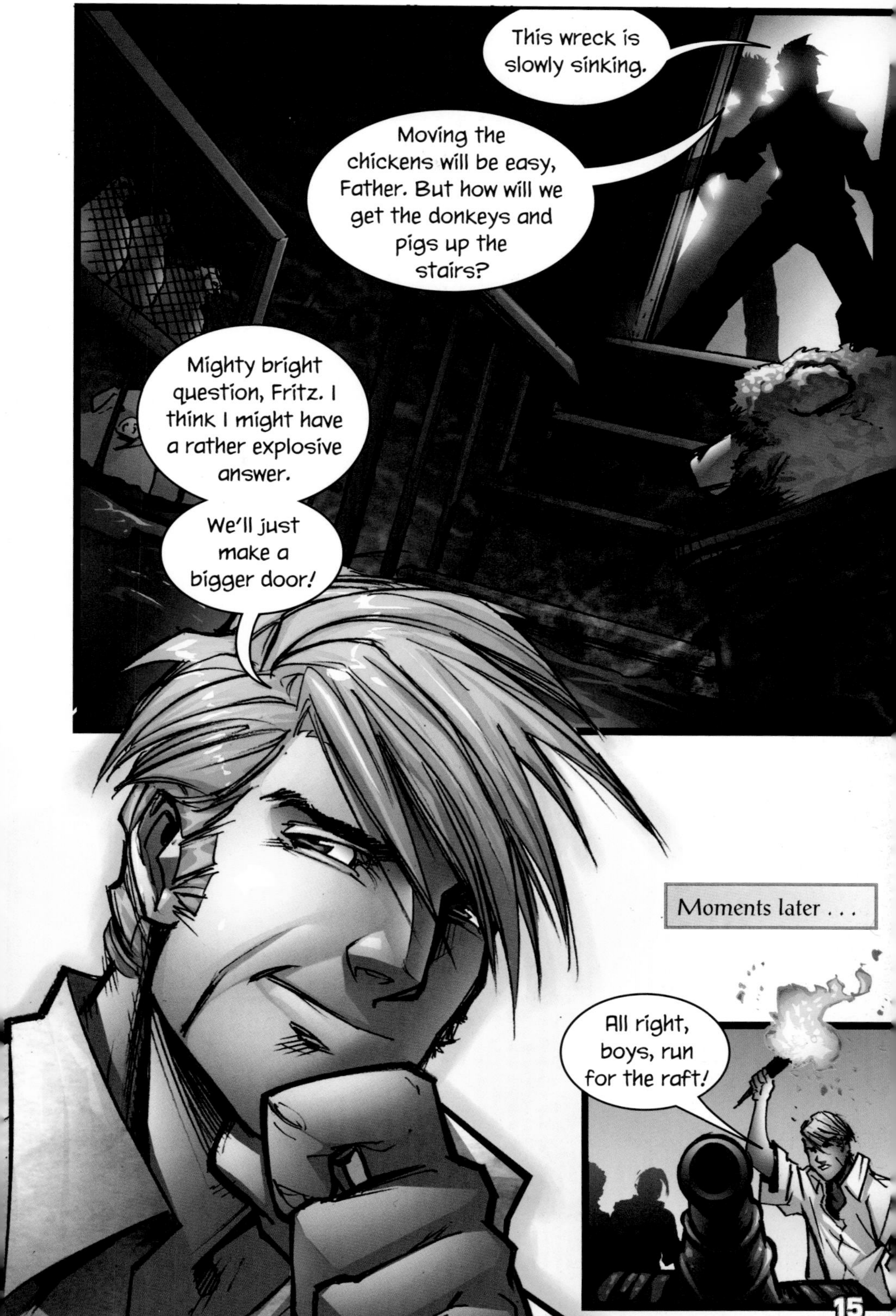
This wreck is slowly sinking.
Moving the chickens will be easy, Father. But how will we get the donkeys and pigs up the stairs?
Mighty bright question, Fritz. I think I might have a rather explosive answer.
We'll just make a bigger door!
Moments later . . .
All right, boys, run for the raft!

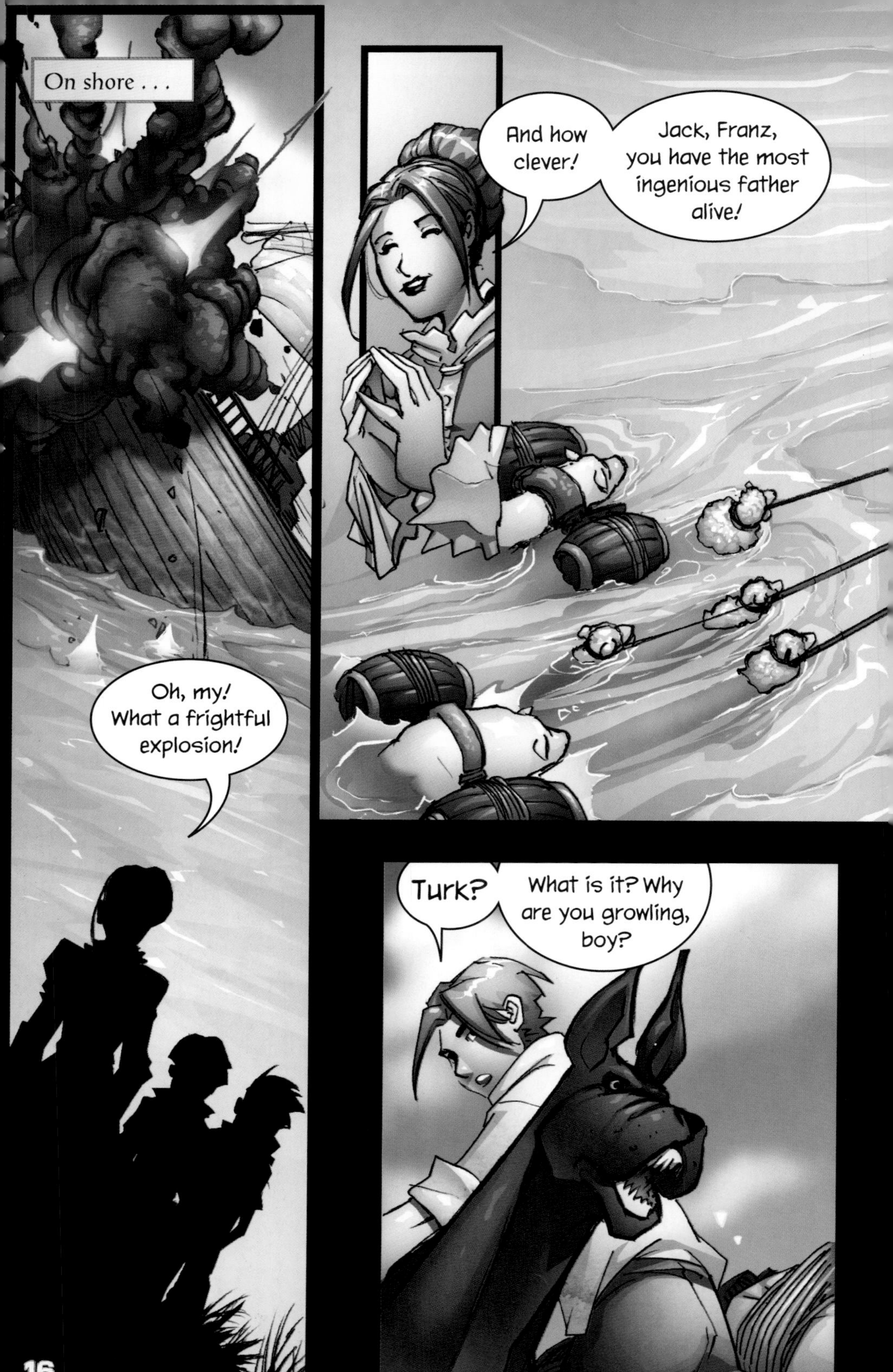
On shore . . .
Oh, my! What a frightful explosion!
And how clever!
Jack, Franz, you have the most ingenious father alive!
Turk?
What is it? Why are you growling, boy?

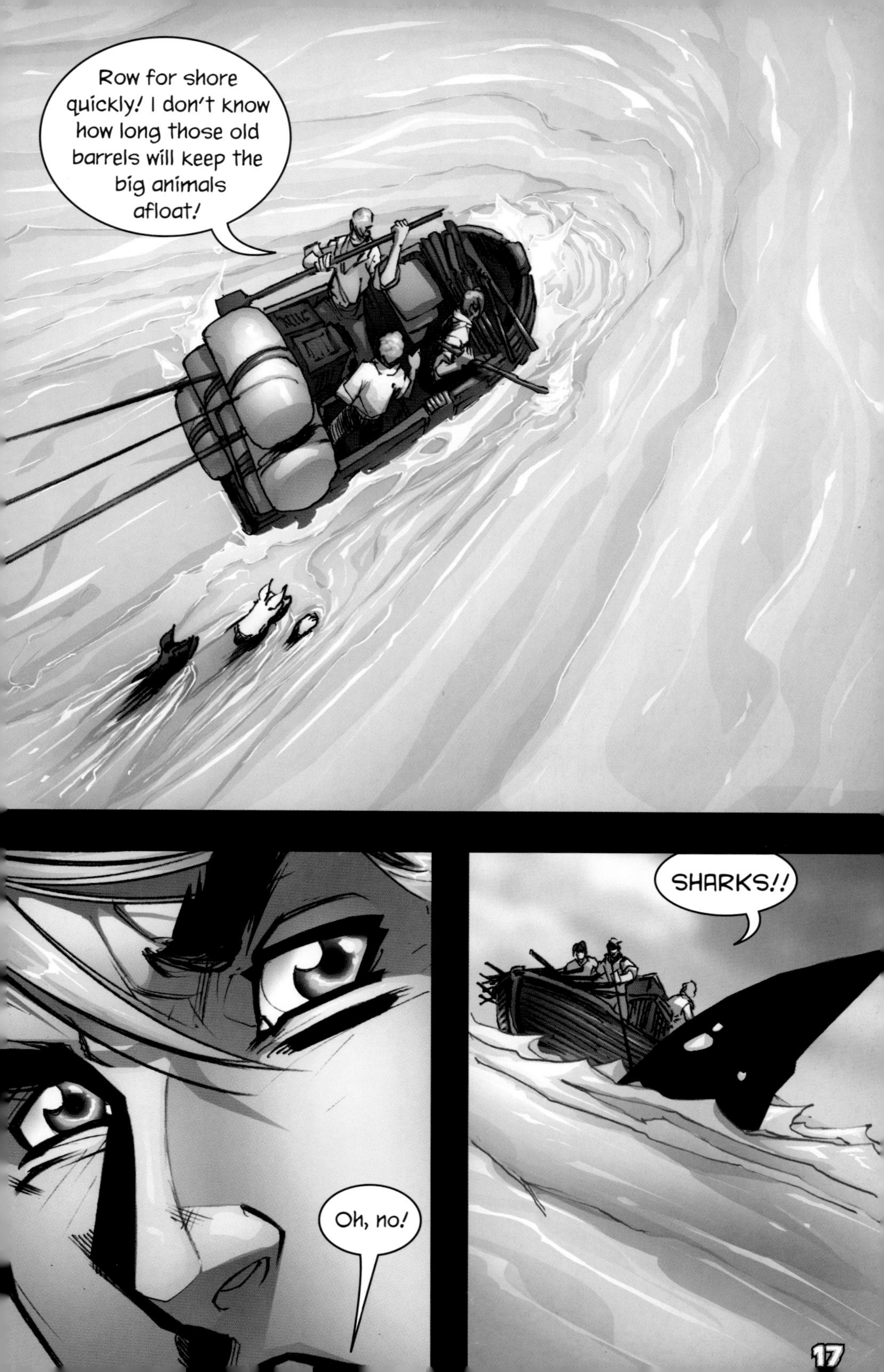
Row for shore quickly! I don't know how long those old barrels will keep the big animals afloat!
Oh, no!
SHARKS!!

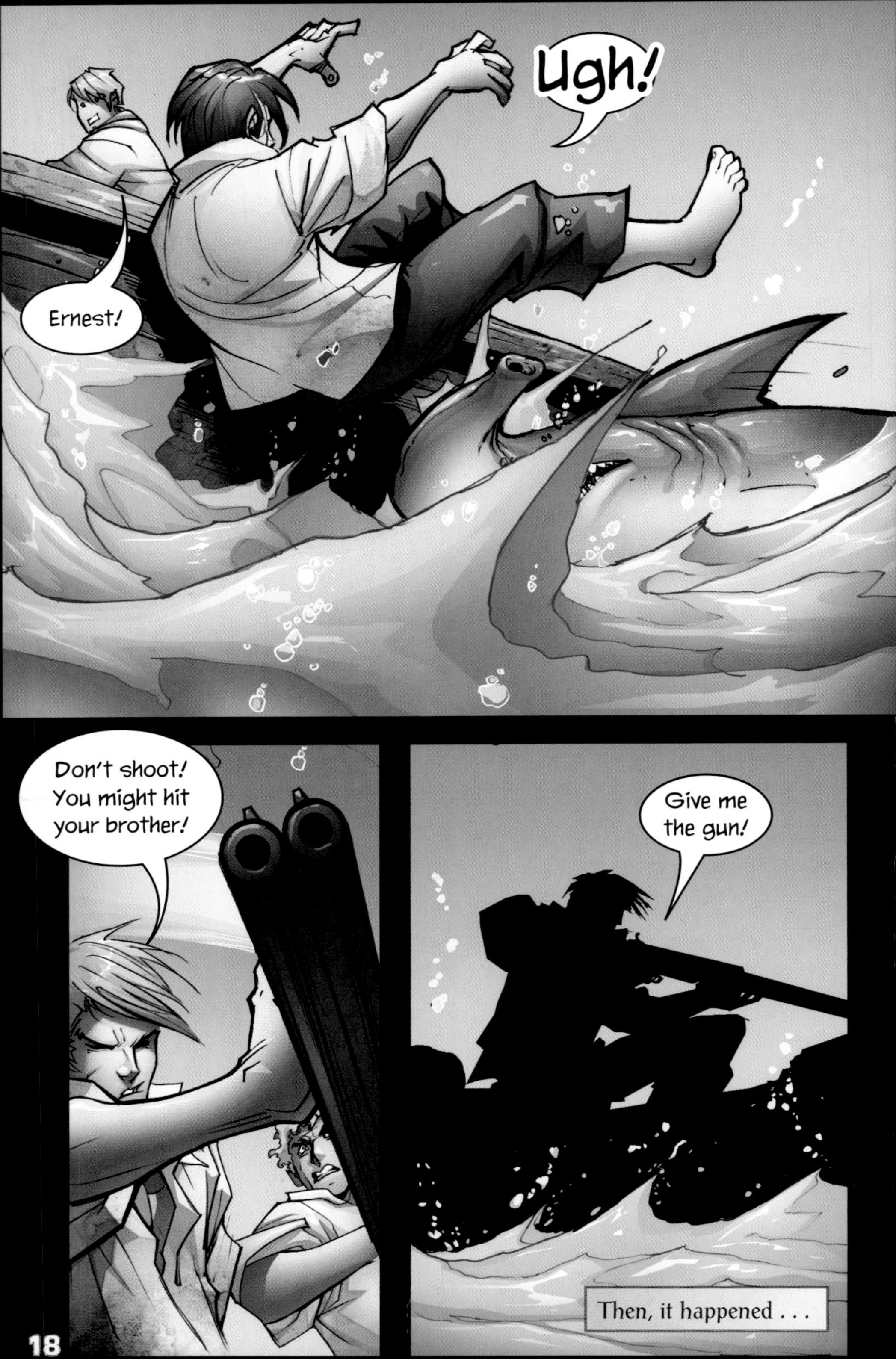

Ugh!
Ernest!
Don't shoot! You might hit your brother!
Give me the gun!
Then, it happened . . .

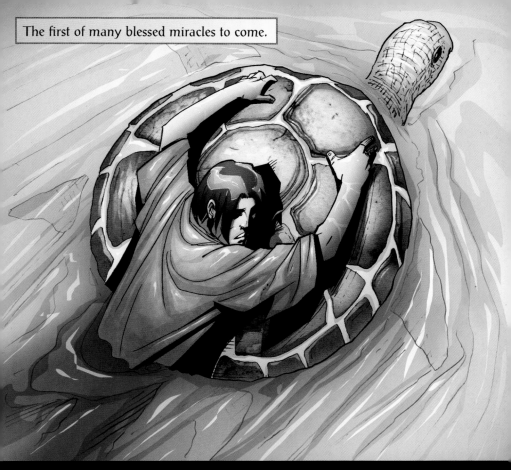

The first of many blessed miracles to come.

Oh, my boy! Thank Heaven you're safe!

It's a loggerhead sea turtle. Look at the size of her!

She swam here to lay her eggs!

19

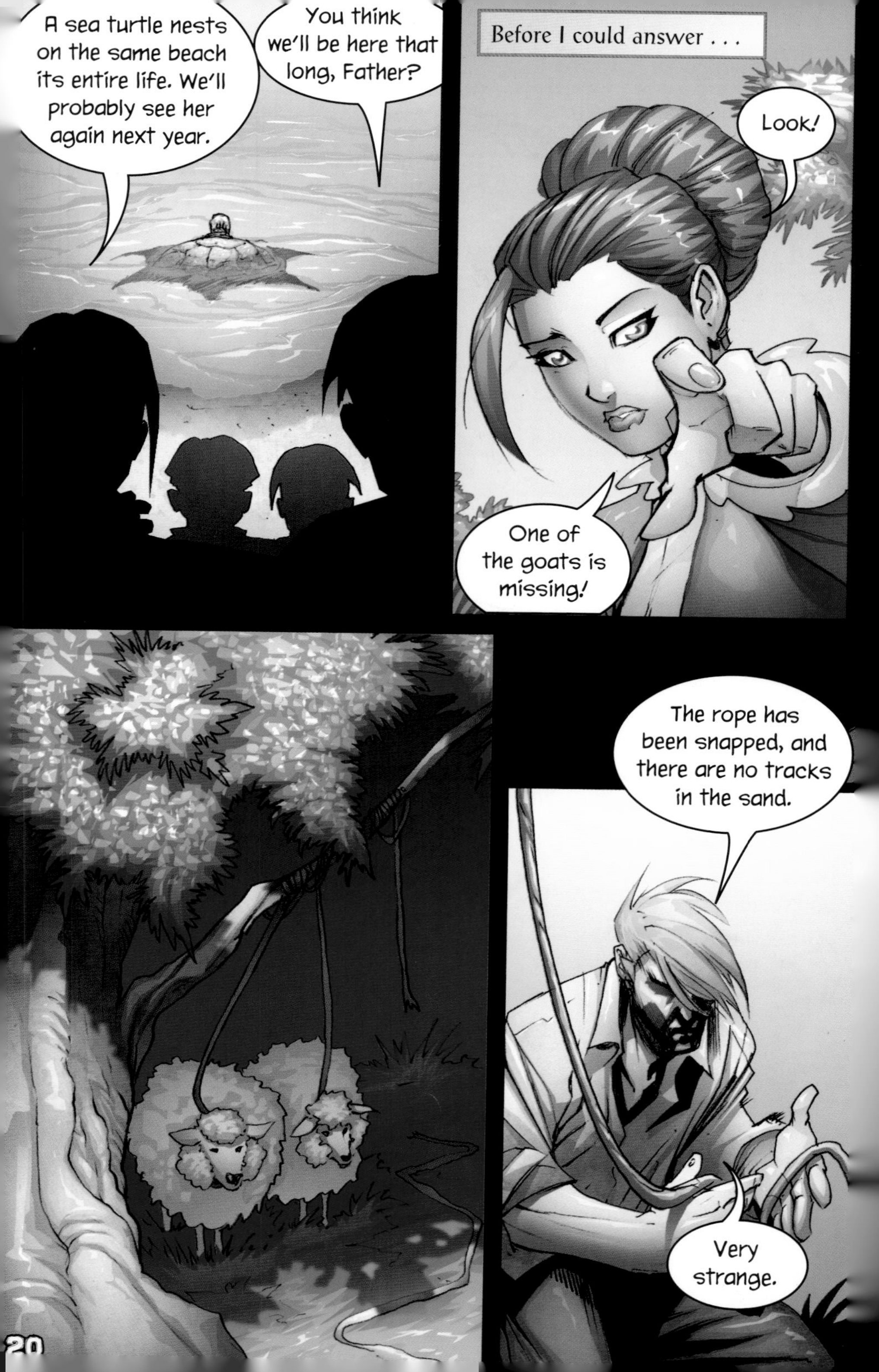
A sea turtle nests on the same beach its entire life. We'll probably see her again next year.
You think we'll be here that long, Father?
Before I could answer . . .
Look!
One of the goats is missing!
The rope has been snapped, and there are no tracks in the sand.
Very strange.

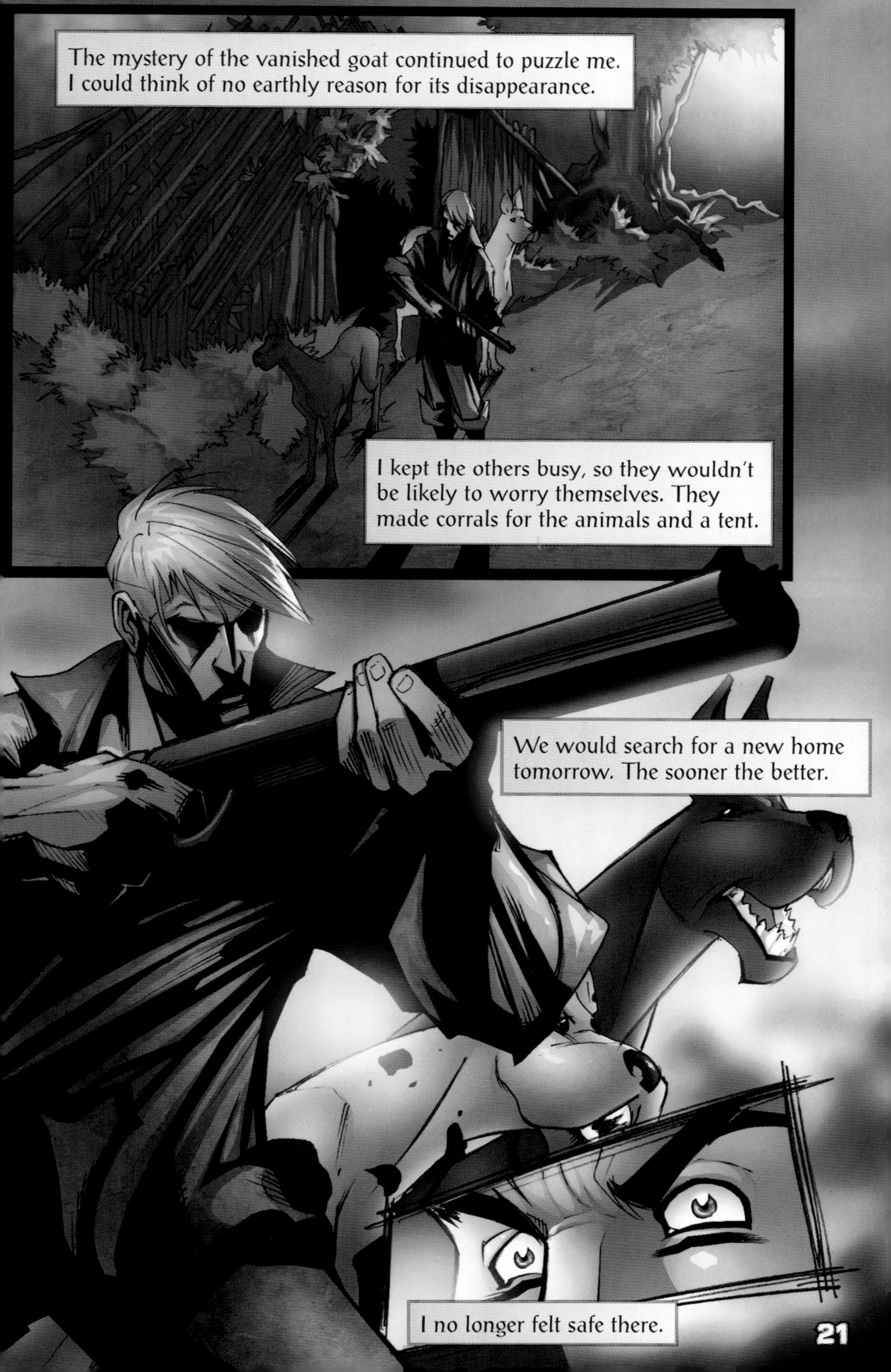
The mystery of the vanished goat continued to puzzle me. I could think of no earthly reason for its disappearance.
I kept the others busy, so they wouldn't be likely to worry themselves. They made corrals for the animals and a tent.
We would search for a new home tomorrow. The sooner the better.
I no longer felt safe there.

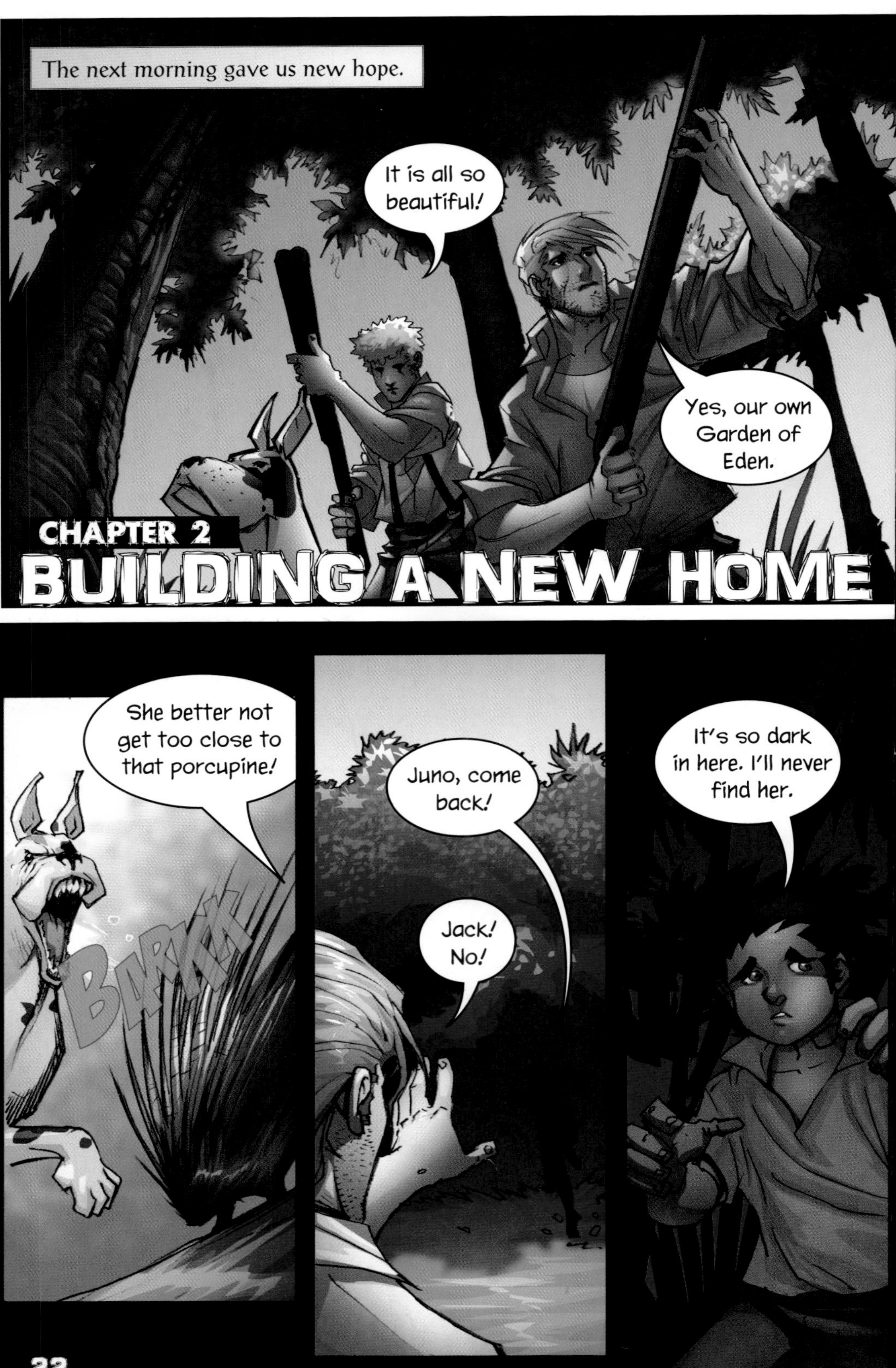
The next morning gave us new hope.
It is all so beautiful!
Yes, our own Garden of Eden.
CHAPTER 2
BUILDING A NEW HOME
She better not get too close to that porcupine!
Juno, come back!
Jack! No!
It's so dark in here. I'll never find her.

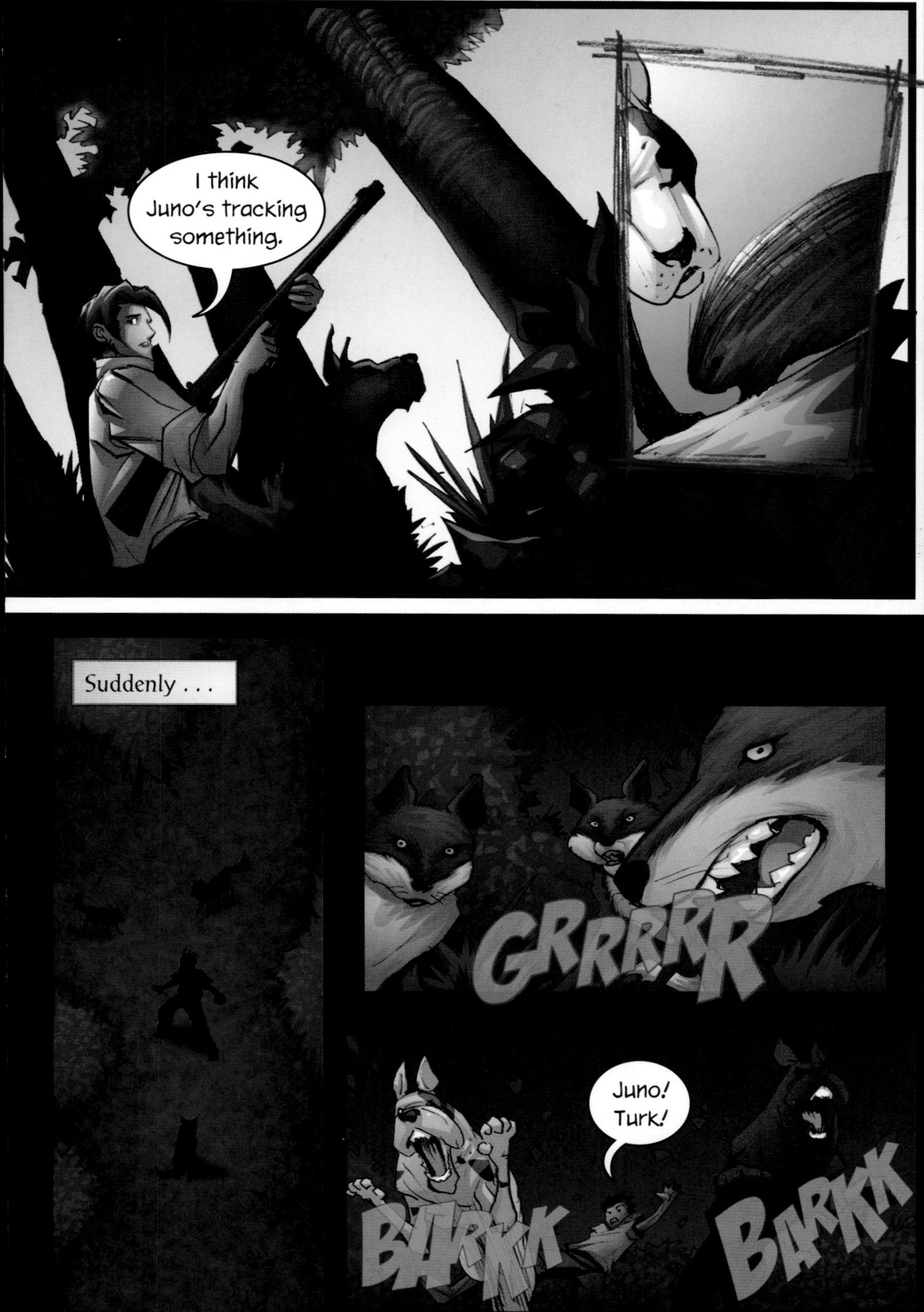
I think Juno's tracking something.
Suddenly . . .
GRRRRR
Juno! Turk!
BARKK
BARKK

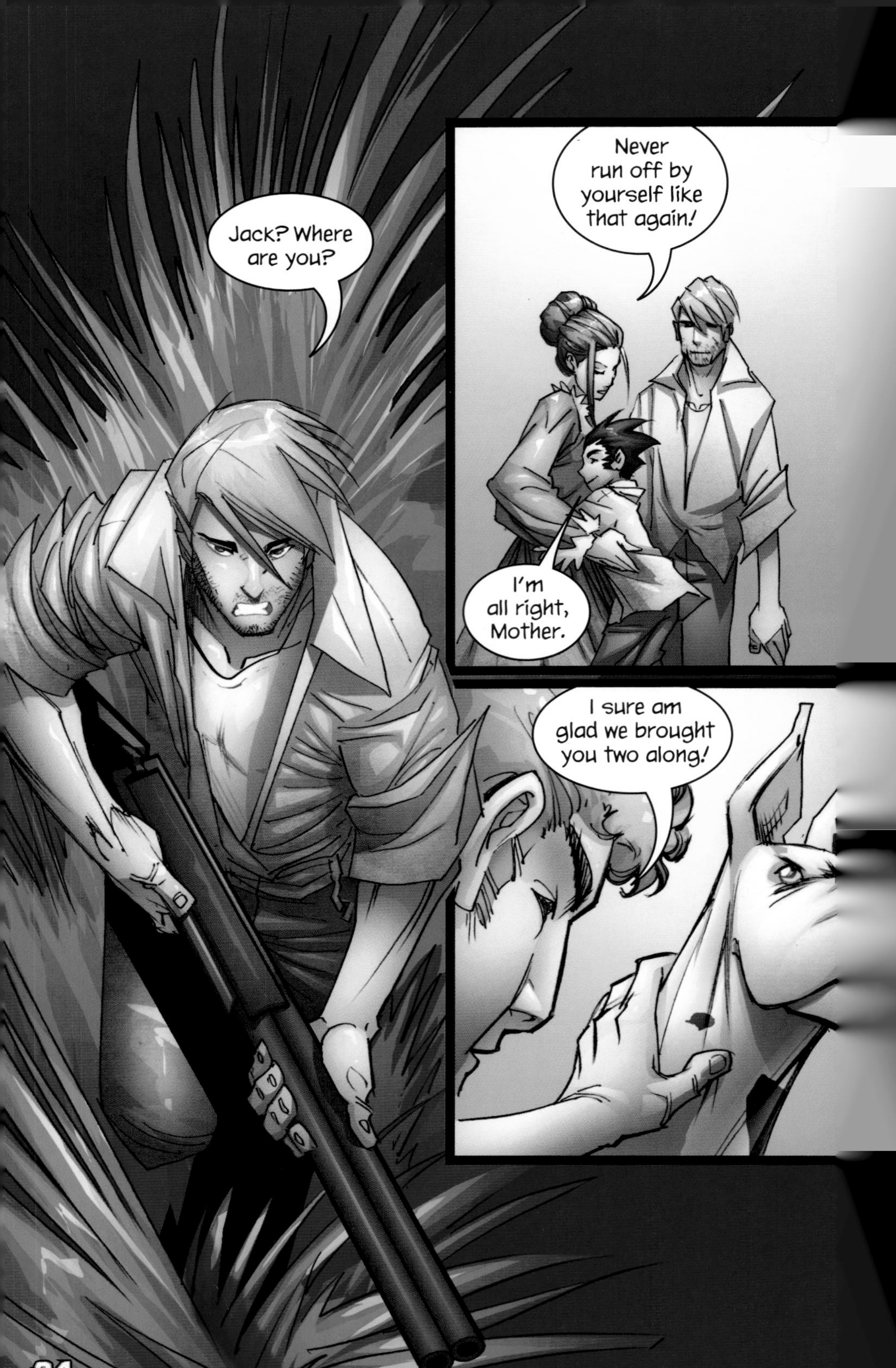
Jack? Where are you?
Never run off by yourself like that again!
I'm all right, Mother.
I sure am glad we brought you two along!

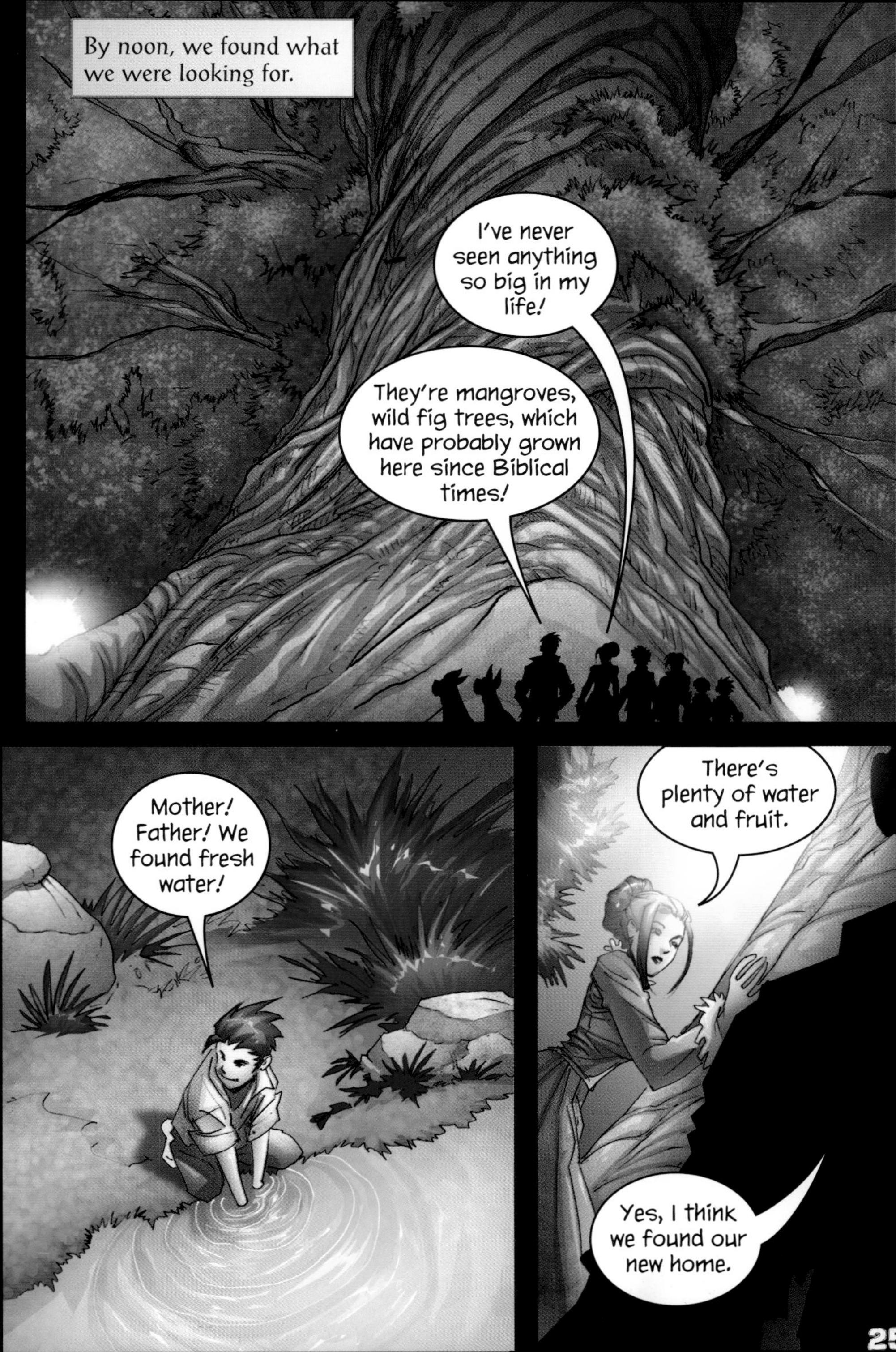
By noon, we found what we were looking for.
I've never seen anything so big in my life!
They're mangroves, wild fig trees, which have probably grown here since Biblical times!
Mother! Father! We found fresh water!
There's plenty of water and fruit.
Yes, I think we found our new home.

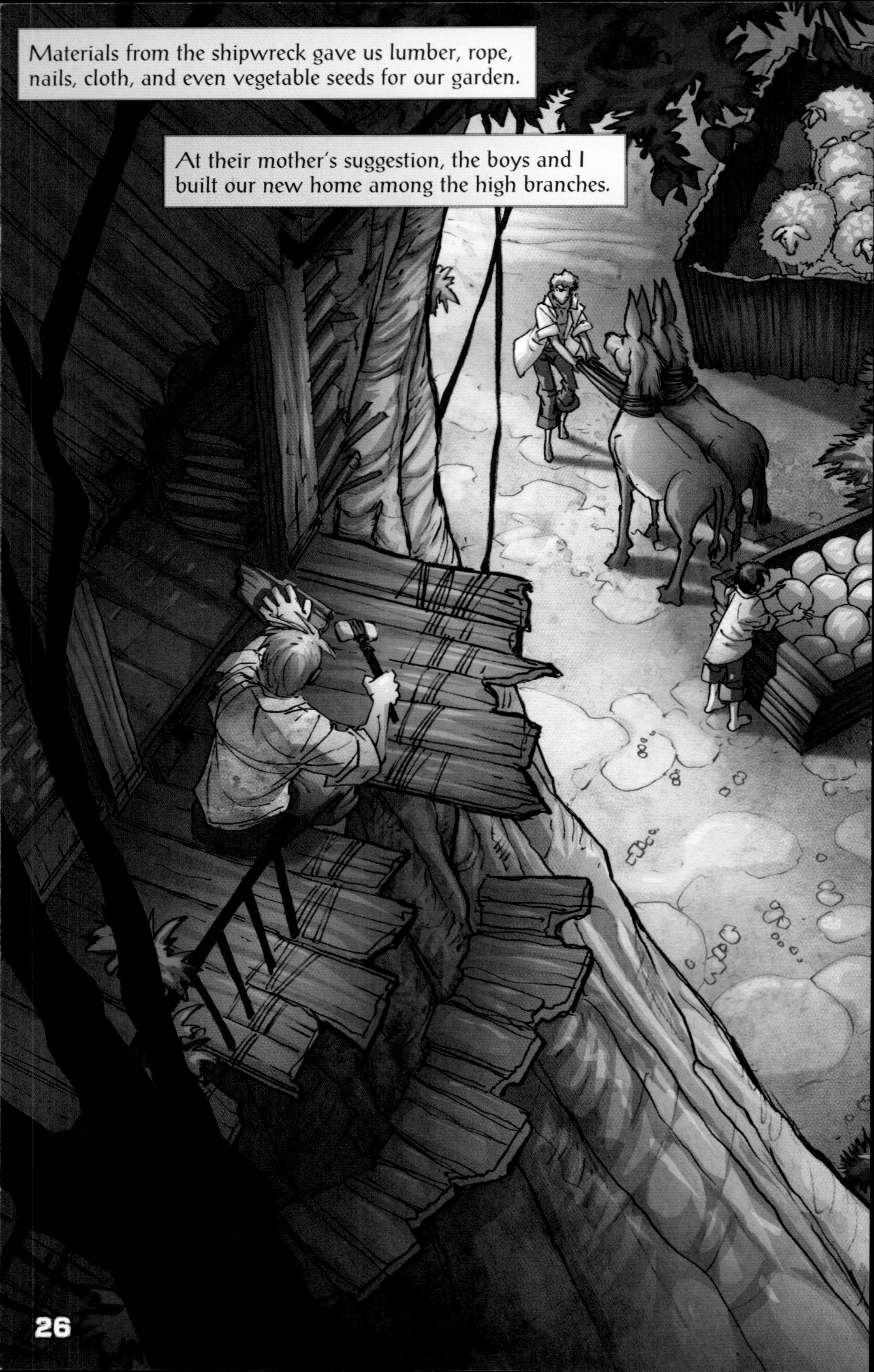
Materials from the shipwreck gave us lumber, rope, nails, cloth, and even vegetable seeds for our garden.
At their mother's suggestion, the boys and I built our new home among the high branches.

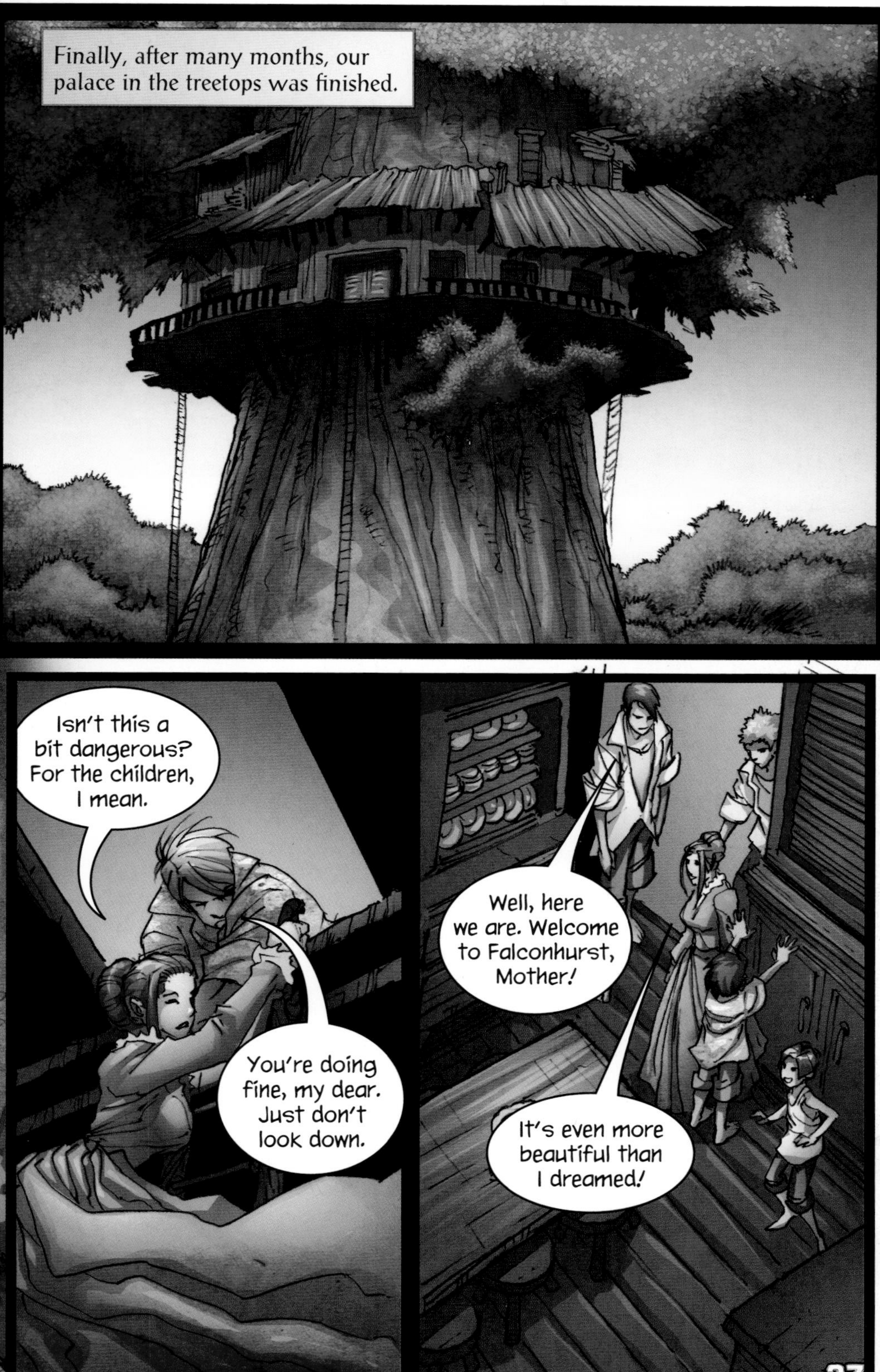
Finally, after many months, our palace in the treetops was finished.
Isn't this a bit dangerous? For the children, I mean.
You're doing fine, my dear. Just don't look down.
Well, here we are. Welcome to Falconhurst, Mother!
It's even more beautiful than I dreamed!

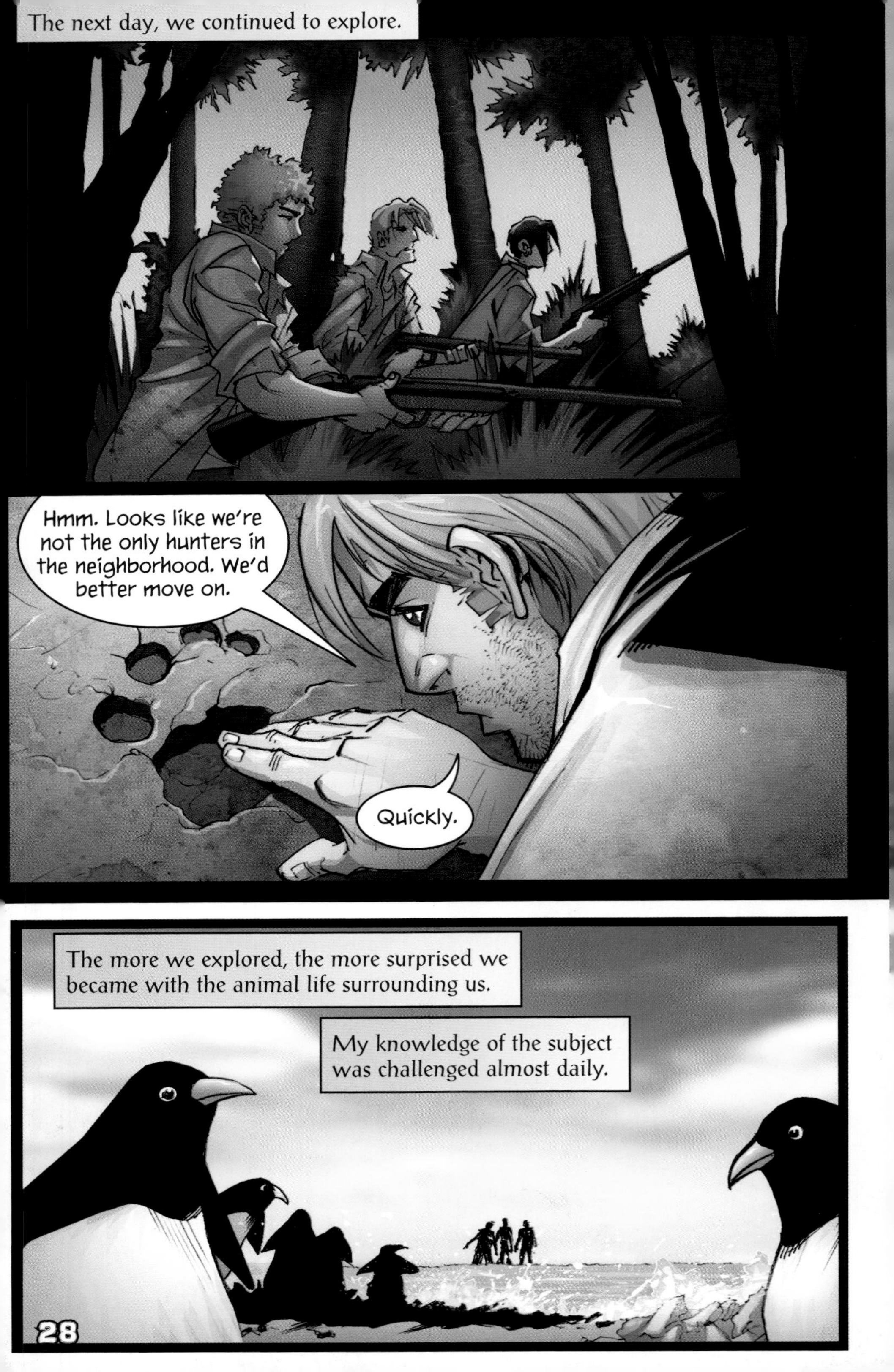
The next day, we continued to explore.
Hmm. Looks like we're not the only hunters in the neighborhood. We'd better move on.
Quickly.
The more we explored, the more surprised we became with the animal life surrounding us.
My knowledge of the subject was challenged almost daily.

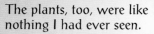

The plants, too, were like nothing I had ever seen.

This is a great discovery! Unless I'm mistaken, it's a manioc root! We can make flour with this!

That means we can have bread!

Yes, now where did those boys run off to?

Father! Mother!

Run for your lives!!

Cape buffalo were the most dangerous beasts of the jungle. The trees were the only safe place from them.

29

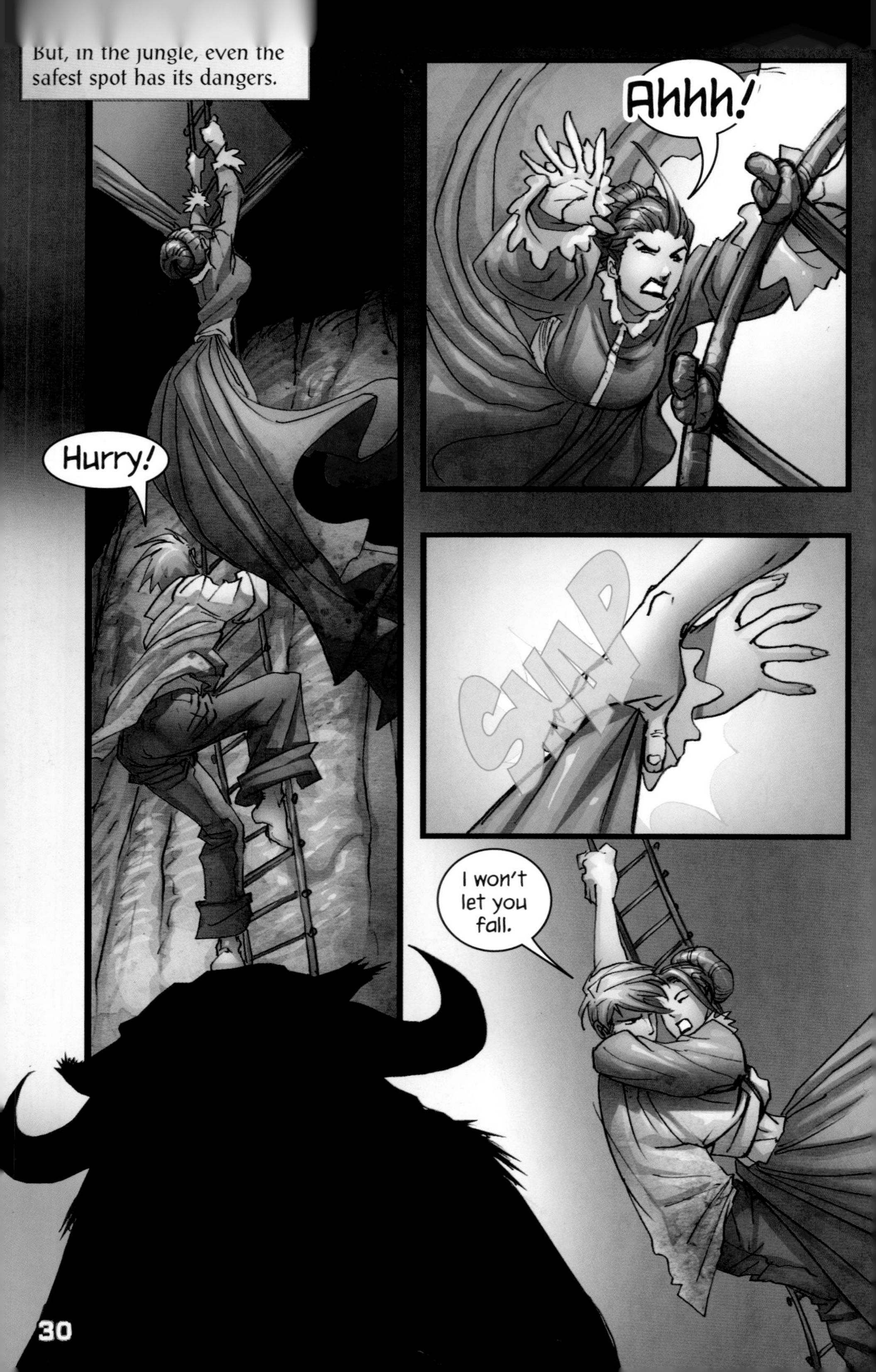
But, in the jungle, even the safest spot has its dangers.
Ahhh!
Hurry!
SNAP
I won't let you fall.

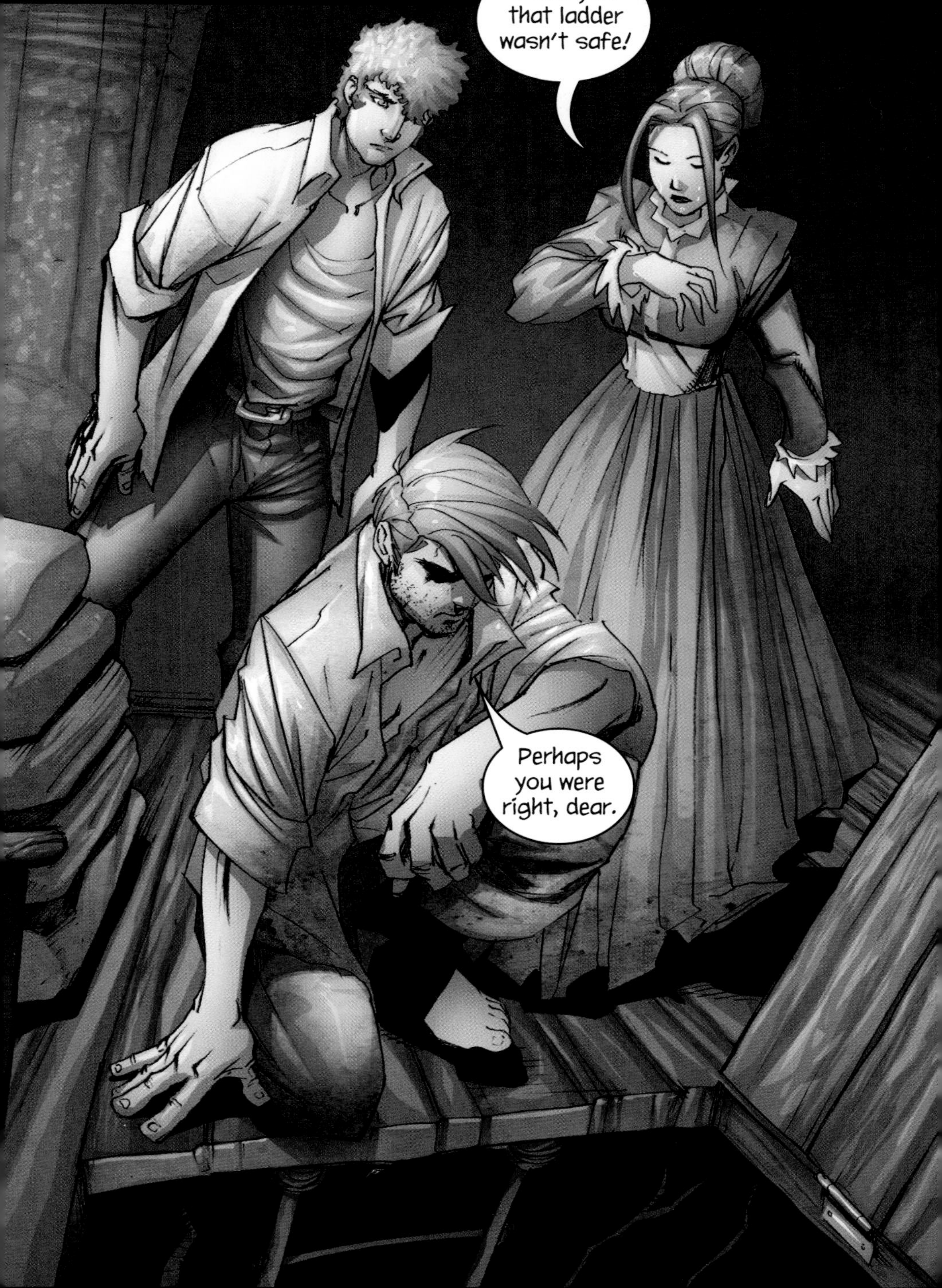
I told you that ladder wasn't safe!
Perhaps you were right, dear.

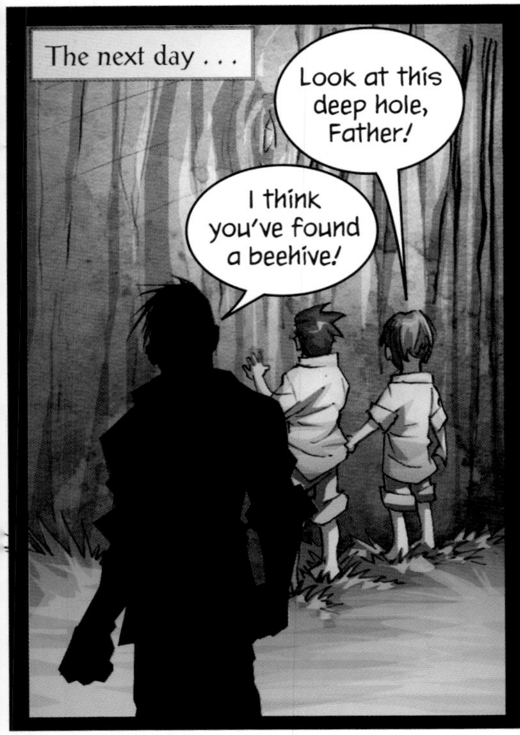
The next day . . .
Look at this deep hole, Father!
I think you've found a beehive!

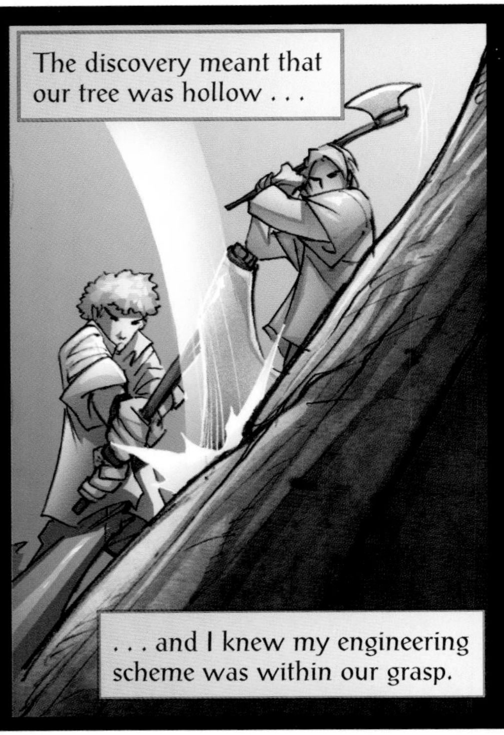
The discovery meant that our tree was hollow . . .
. . . and I knew my engineering scheme was within our grasp.

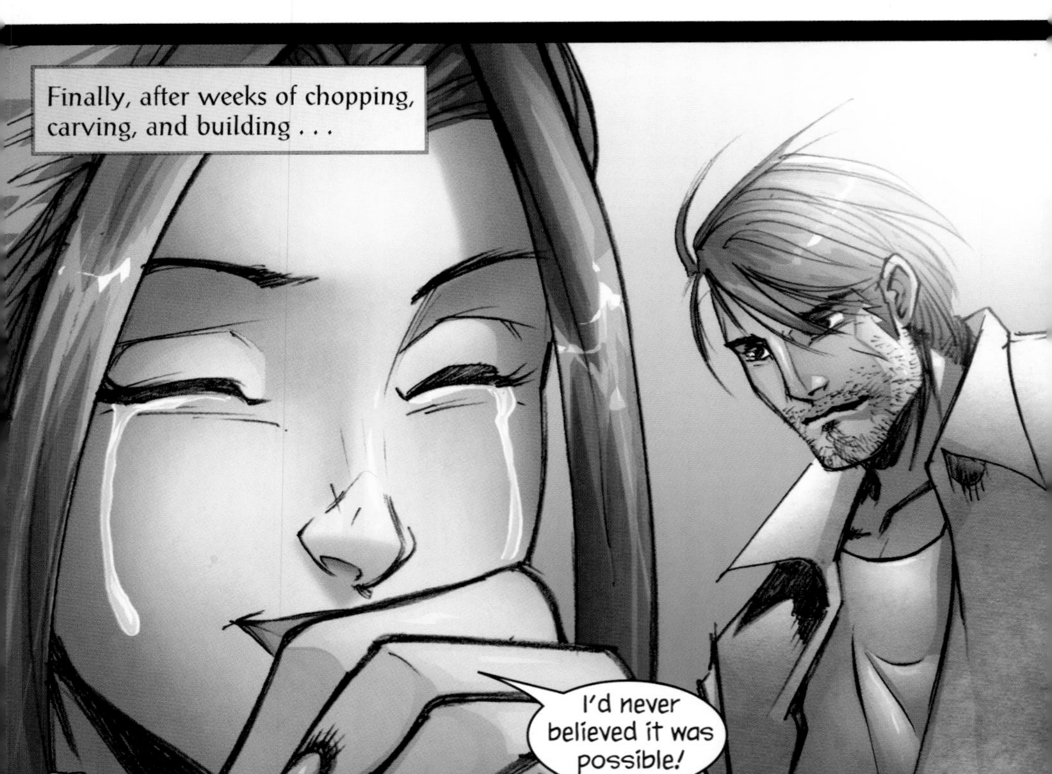
Finally, after weeks of chopping, carving, and building . . .
I'd never believed it was possible!

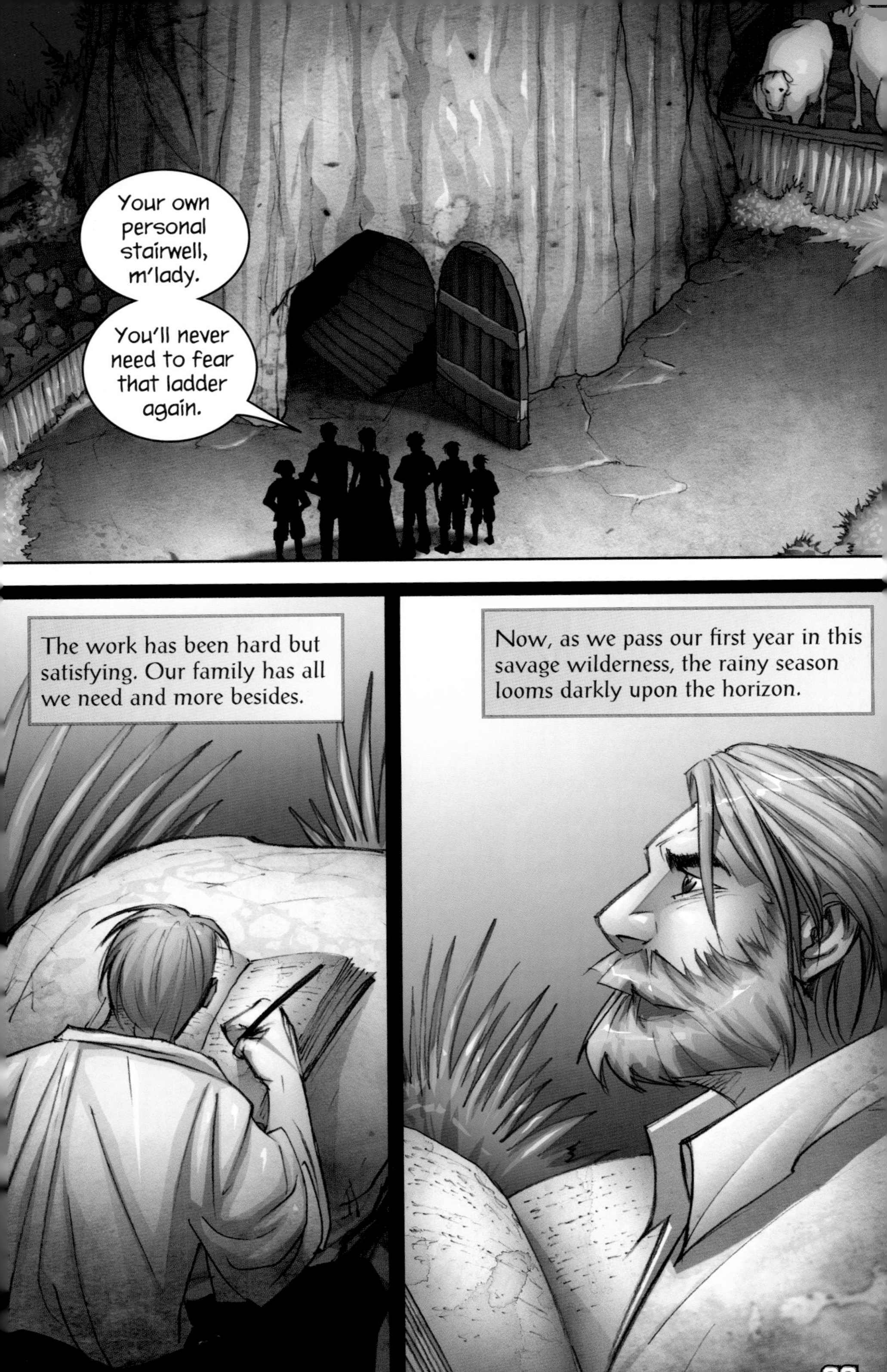
Your own personal stairwell, m'lady.
You'll never need to fear that ladder again.
The work has been hard but satisfying. Our family has all we need and more besides.
Now, as we pass our first year in this savage wilderness, the rainy season looms darkly upon the horizon.

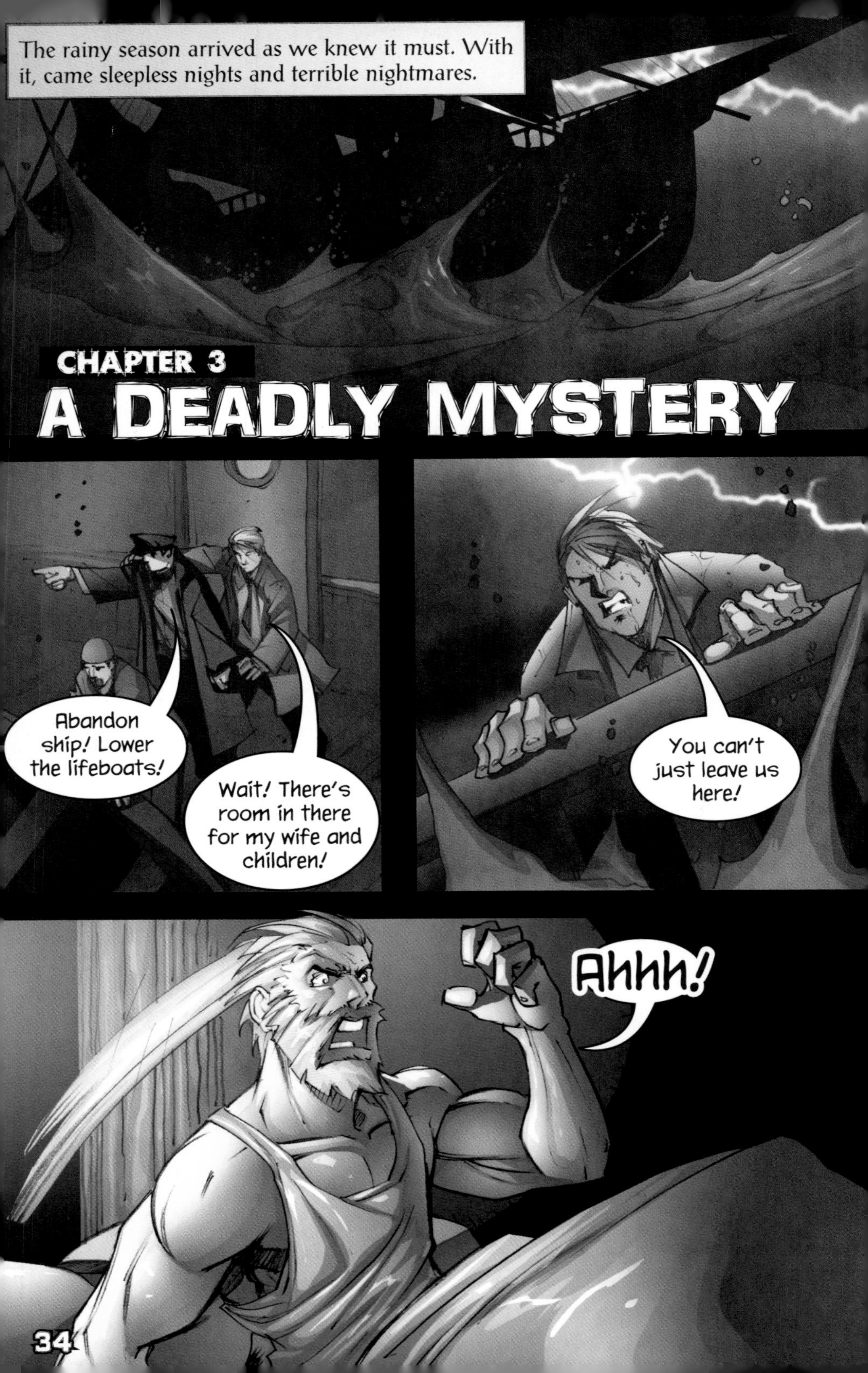
The rainy season arrived as we knew it must. With it, came sleepless nights and terrible nightmares.
CHAPTER 3
A DEADLY MYSTERY
Abandon ship! Lower the lifeboats!
Wait! There's room in there for my wife and children!
You can't just leave us here!
Ahhh!

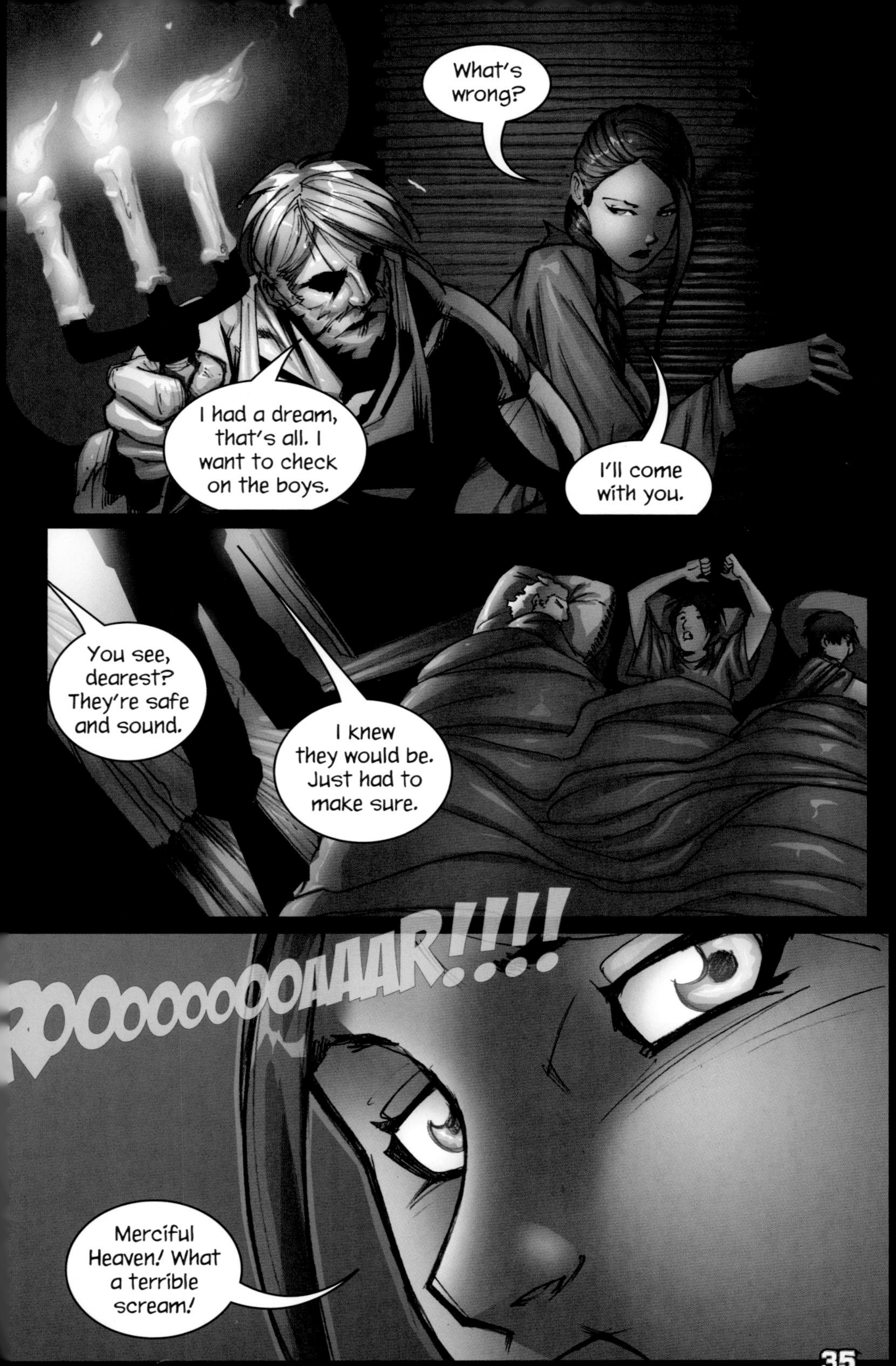
What's wrong?
I had a dream, that's all. I want to check on the boys.
I'll come with you.
You see, dearest? They're safe and sound.
I knew they would be. Just had to make sure.
ROOOOOOOOAAAR!!!!
Merciful Heaven! What a terrible scream!

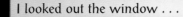

It's a tiger! I see it prowling below in the rain!

It's all right, Mother. We made the new corral very strong. The tiger cannot get to the animals.

The beast must be after the livestock! You must kill it!

May we look at the tiger, Father?

I might only wound it, and an injured tiger would be even more dangerous.

36

You'll see him soon enough. It's back to bed for all of us. Let's get what rest we can.
There's a tiger to hunt in the morning.
ROOOOOOOOAAAR!!!!

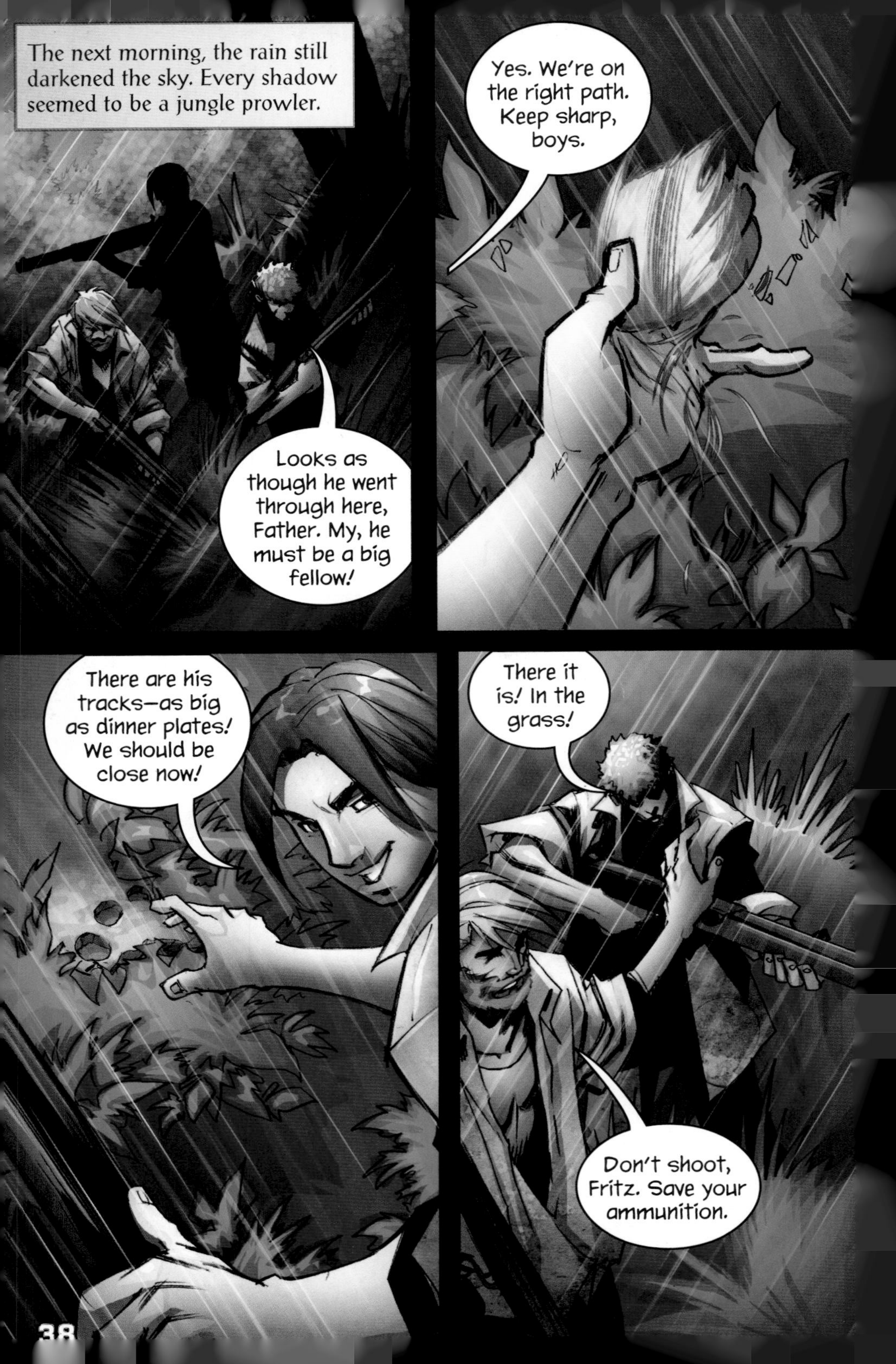
The next morning, the rain still darkened the sky. Every shadow seemed to be a jungle prowler.
Looks as though he went through here, Father. My, he must be a big fellow!
Yes. We're on the right path. Keep sharp, boys.
There are his tracks—as big as dinner plates! We should be close now!
There it is! In the grass!
Don't shoot, Fritz. Save your ammunition.

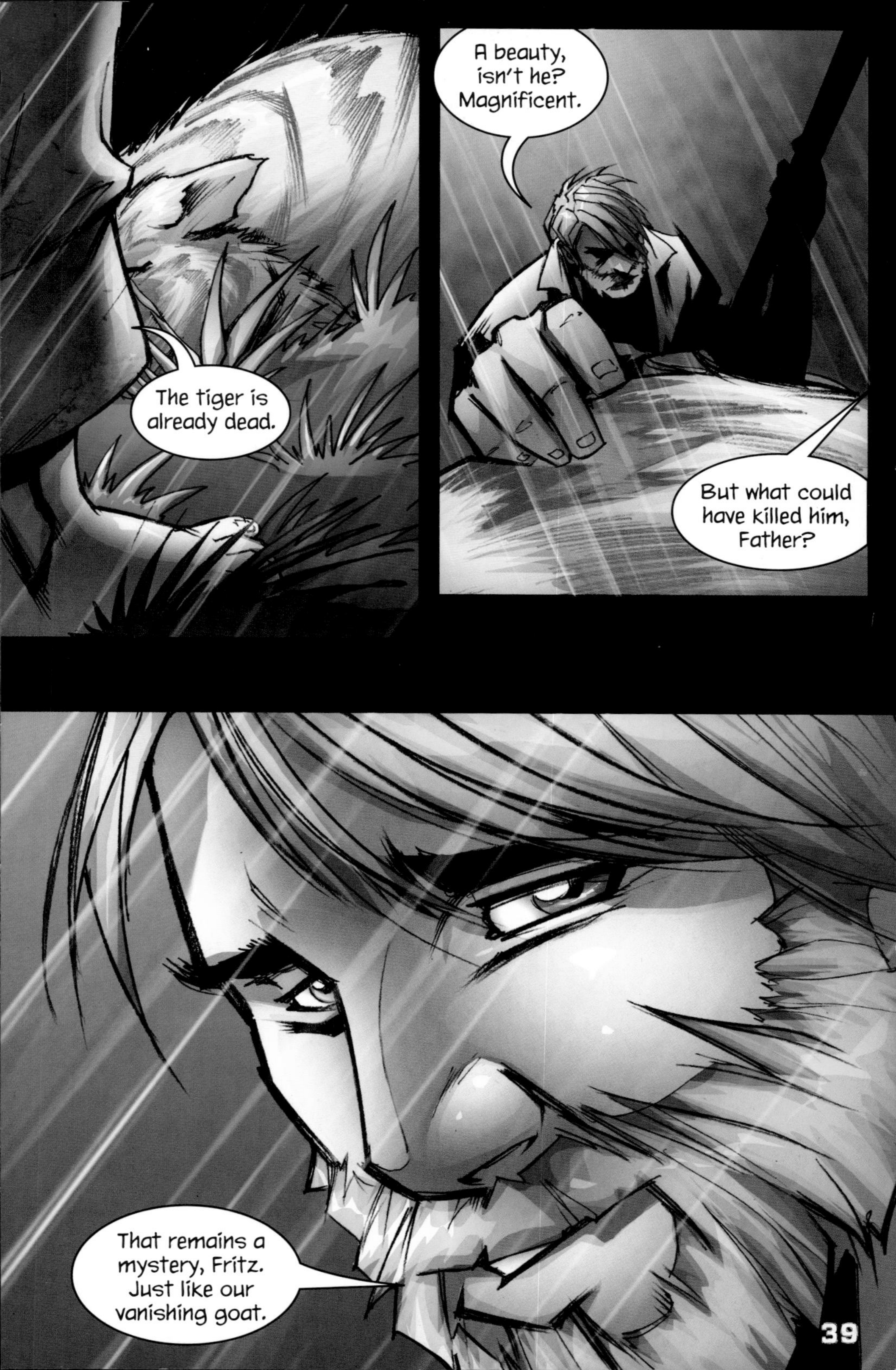
The tiger is already dead.
A beauty, isn't he? Magnificent.
But what could have killed him, Father?
That remains a mystery, Fritz. Just like our vanishing goat.

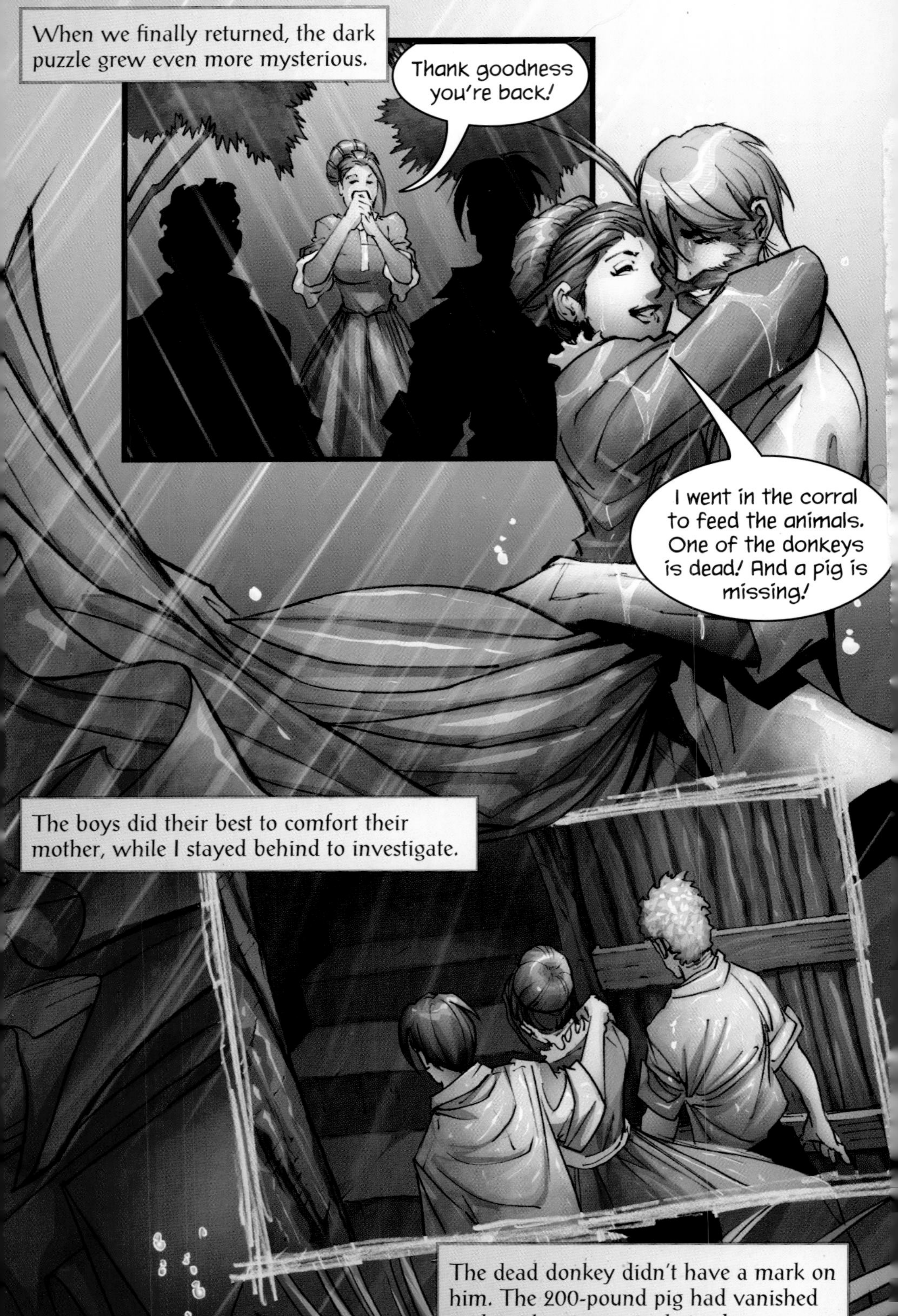
When we finally returned, the dark puzzle grew even more mysterious.
Thank goodness you're back!
I went in the corral to feed the animals. One of the donkeys is dead! And a pig is missing!
The boys did their best to comfort their mother, while I stayed behind to investigate.
The dead donkey didn't have a mark on him. The 200-pound pig had vanished without leaving a single track.

And, still the rain drove down upon us without end.

Indeed, as curtains of rain came down, we each raised the spirits of the others.

We celebrated Christmas, finding strength and peace in old hymns and prayers.

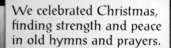

Outside, the rainstorms continued, but within we shared a deep togetherness of which other families can only dream.

In spite of fear, my family was a happy one.

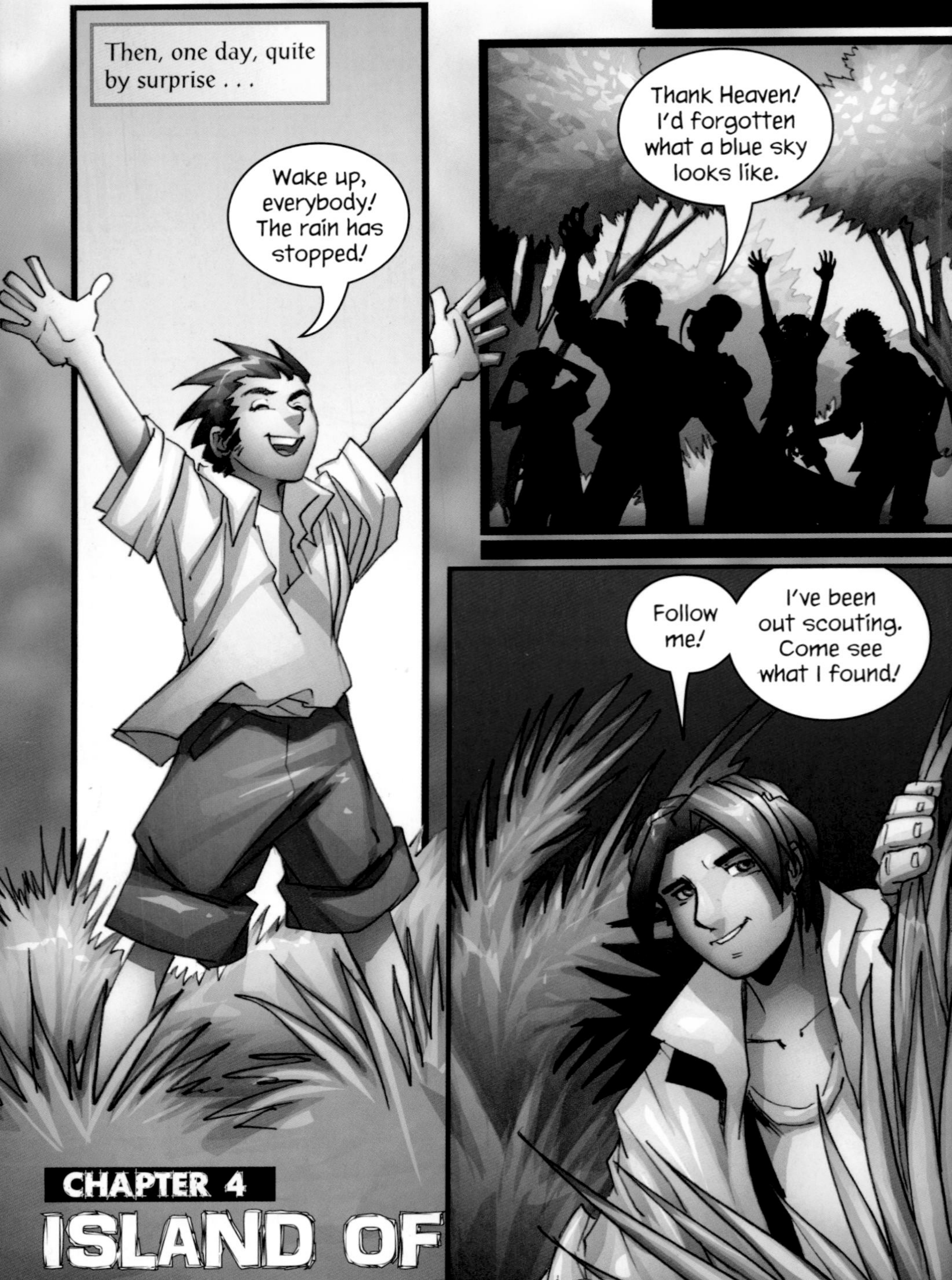

Then, one day, quite by surprise . . .
Wake up, everybody! The rain has stopped!
Thank Heaven! I'd forgotten what a blue sky looks like.
Follow me!
I've been out scouting. Come see what I found!

CHAPTER 4
ISLAND OF GOOD FORTUNE

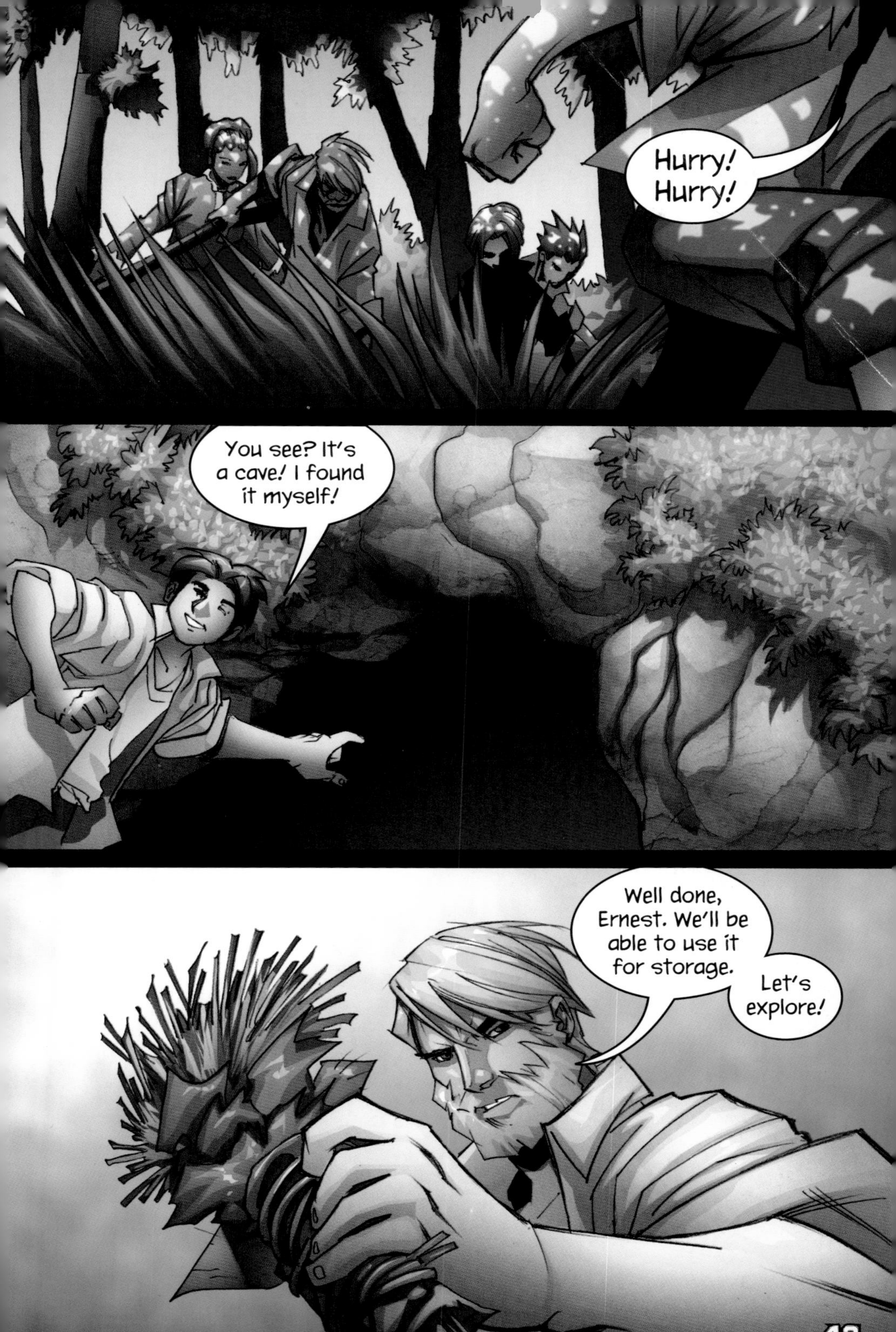
Hurry! Hurry!
You see? It's a cave! I found it myself!
Well done, Ernest. We'll be able to use it for storage.
Let's explore!

A cave of rock salt.
It must have been carved for us by this stream, which was once a mighty river long, long ago.
It's perfect. This will be our new winter home!

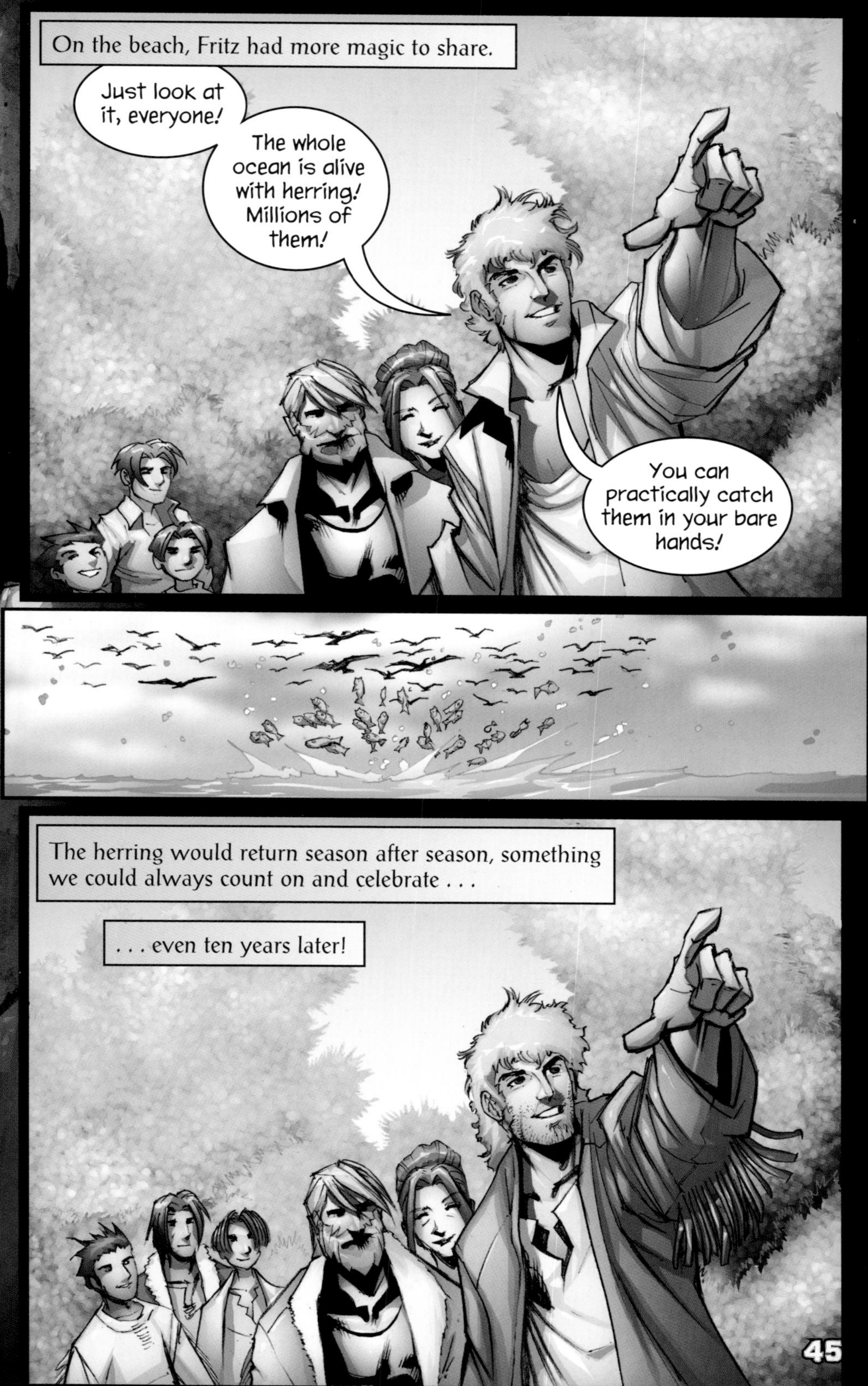
On the beach, Fritz had more magic to share.
Just look at it, everyone!
The whole ocean is alive with herring! Millions of them!
You can practically catch them in your bare hands!
The herring would return season after season, something we could always count on and celebrate . . .
. . . even ten years later!

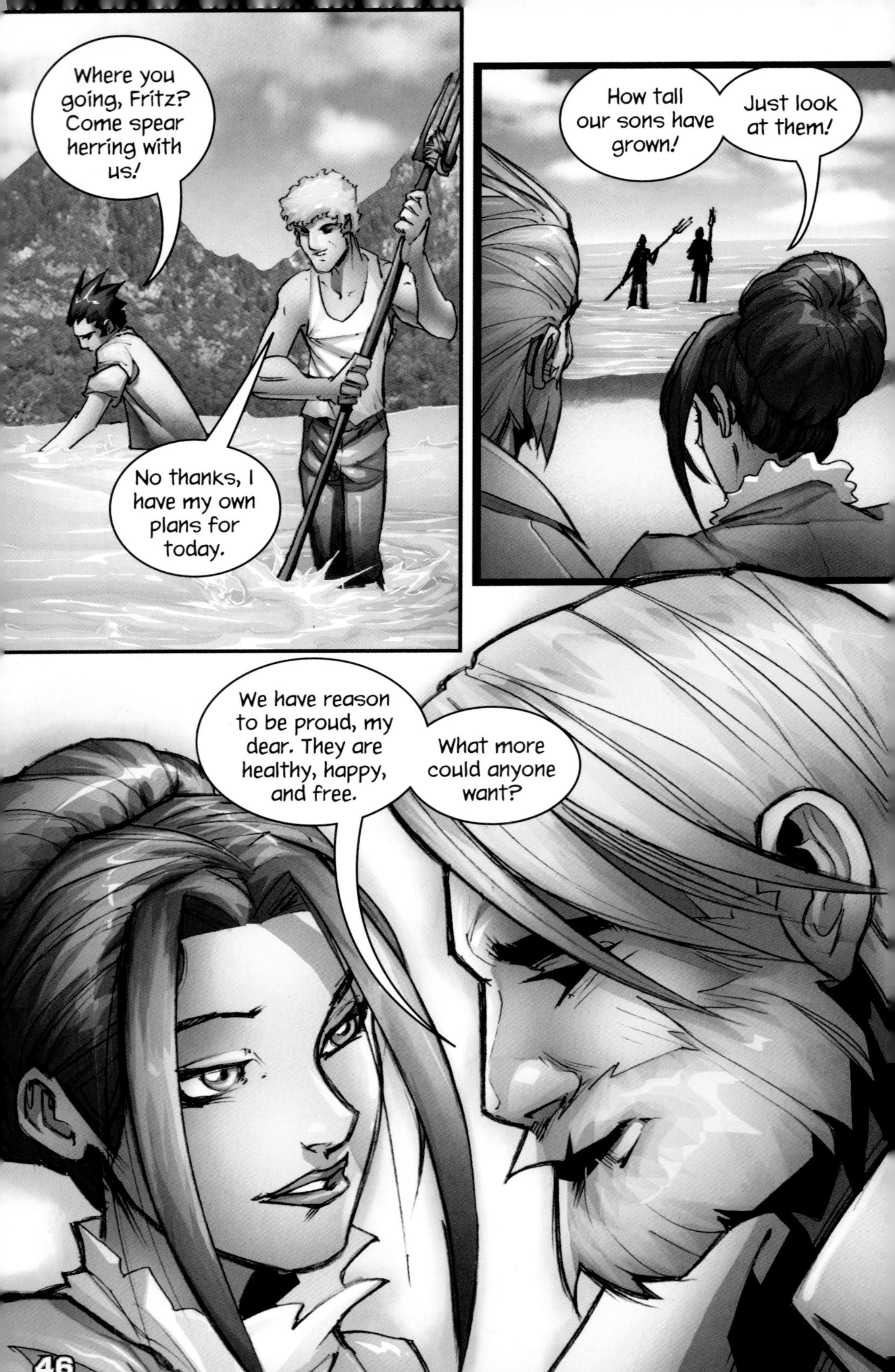
Where you going, Fritz? Come spear herring with us!
No thanks, I have my own plans for today.
How tall our sons have grown!
Just look at them!
We have reason to be proud, my dear. They are healthy, happy, and free.
What more could anyone want?

CHAPTER 5
FRITZ'S DISCOVERY

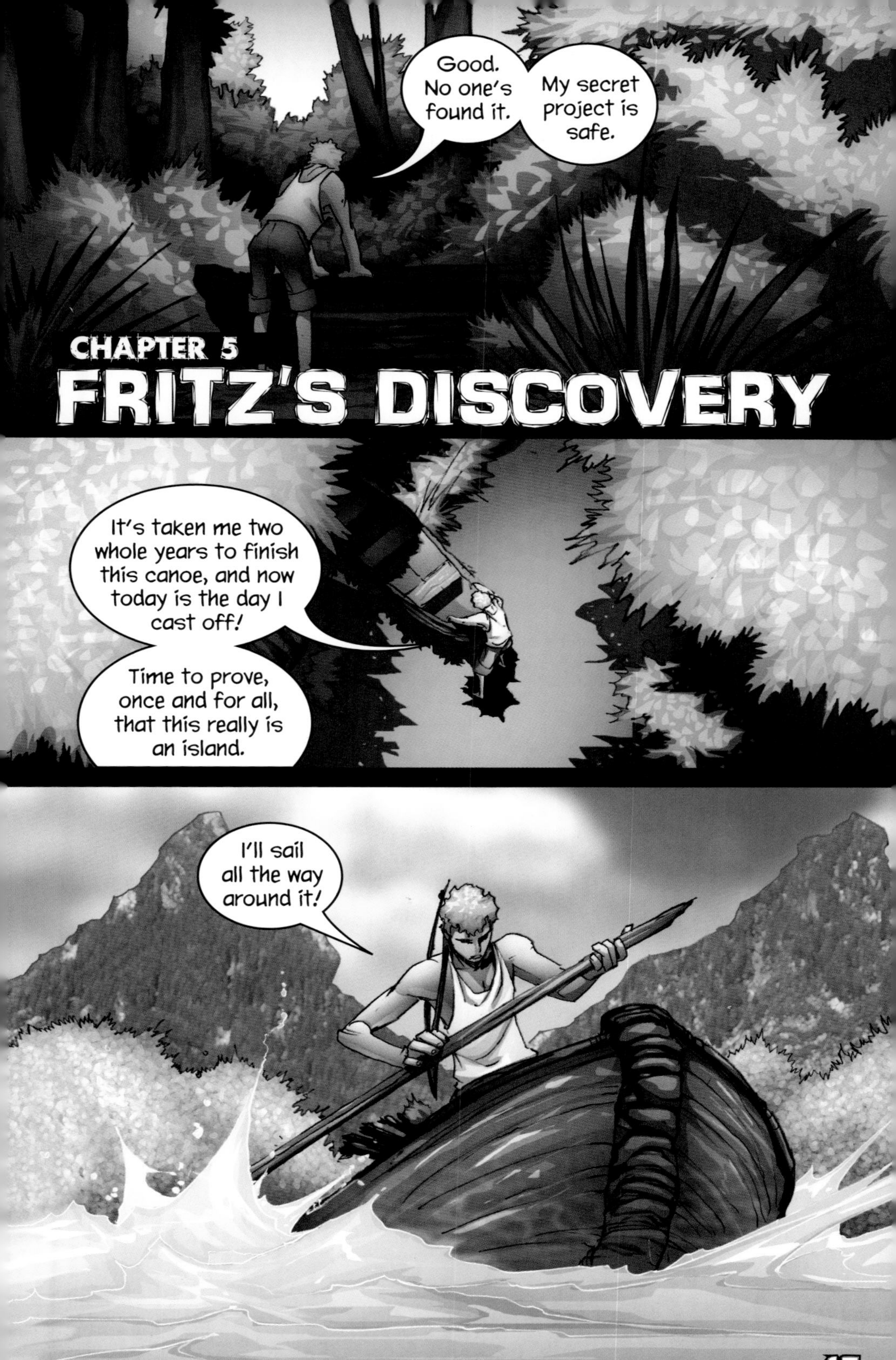
Good. No one's found it.
My secret project is safe.
It's taken me two whole years to finish this canoe, and now today is the day I cast off!
Time to prove, once and for all, that this really is an island.
I'll sail all the way around it!

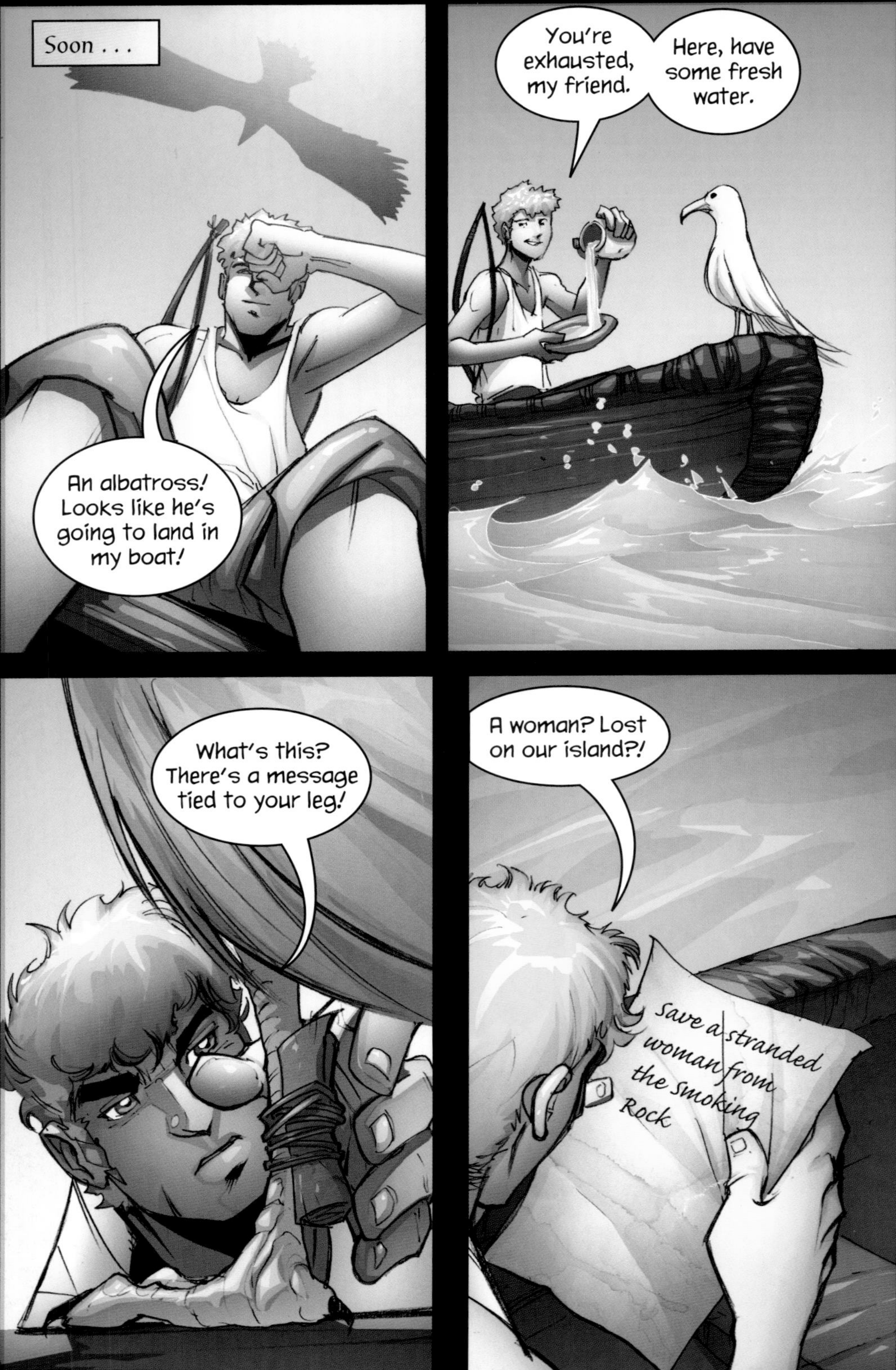
Soon . . .
An albatross! Looks like he's going to land in my boat!
You're exhausted, my friend.
Here, have some fresh water.
What's this? There's a message tied to your leg!
A woman? Lost on our island?!
Save a stranded woman from the Smoking Rock

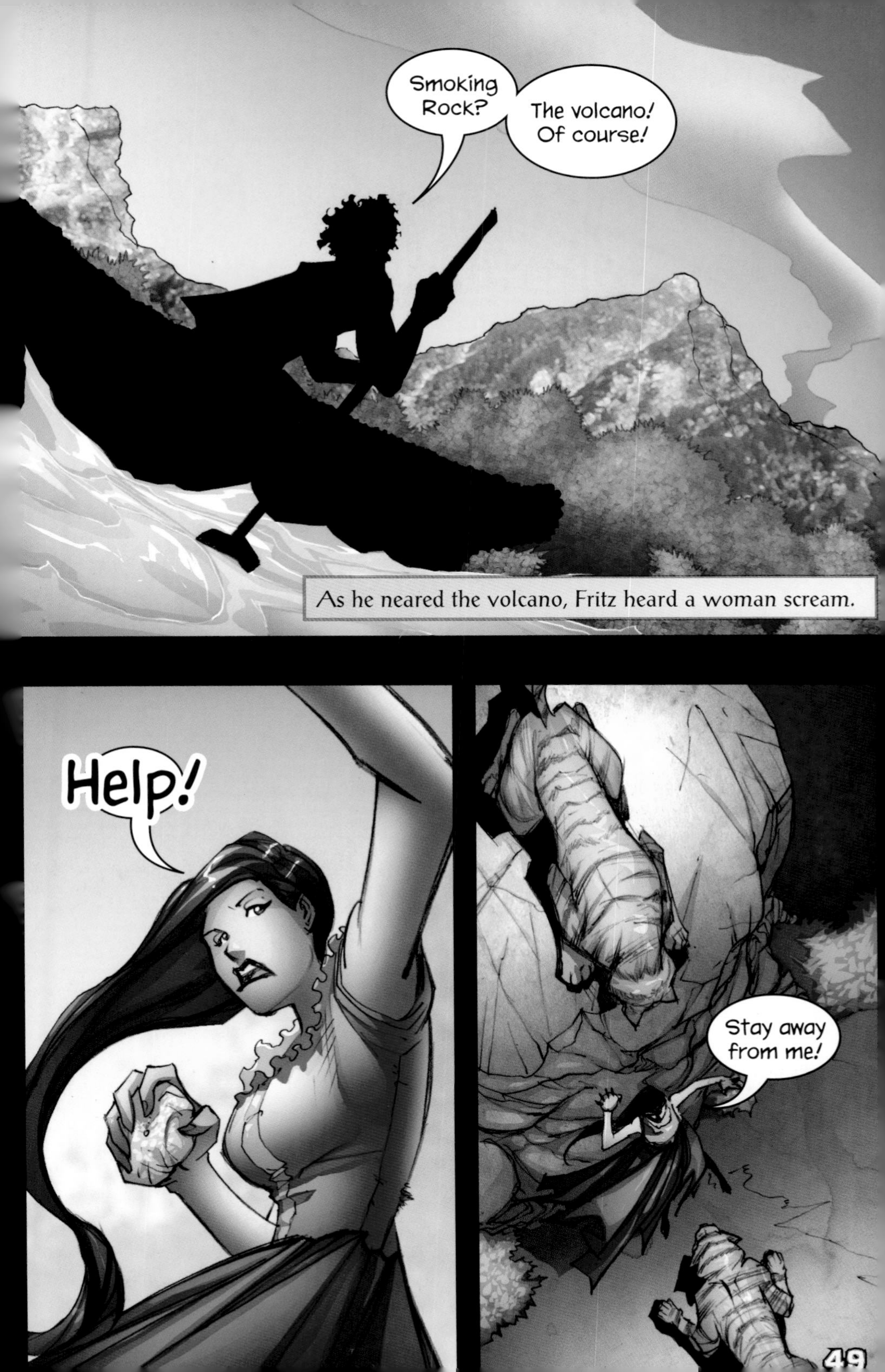
Smoking Rock?
The volcano! Of course!
As he neared the volcano, Fritz heard a woman scream.
Help!
Stay away from me!

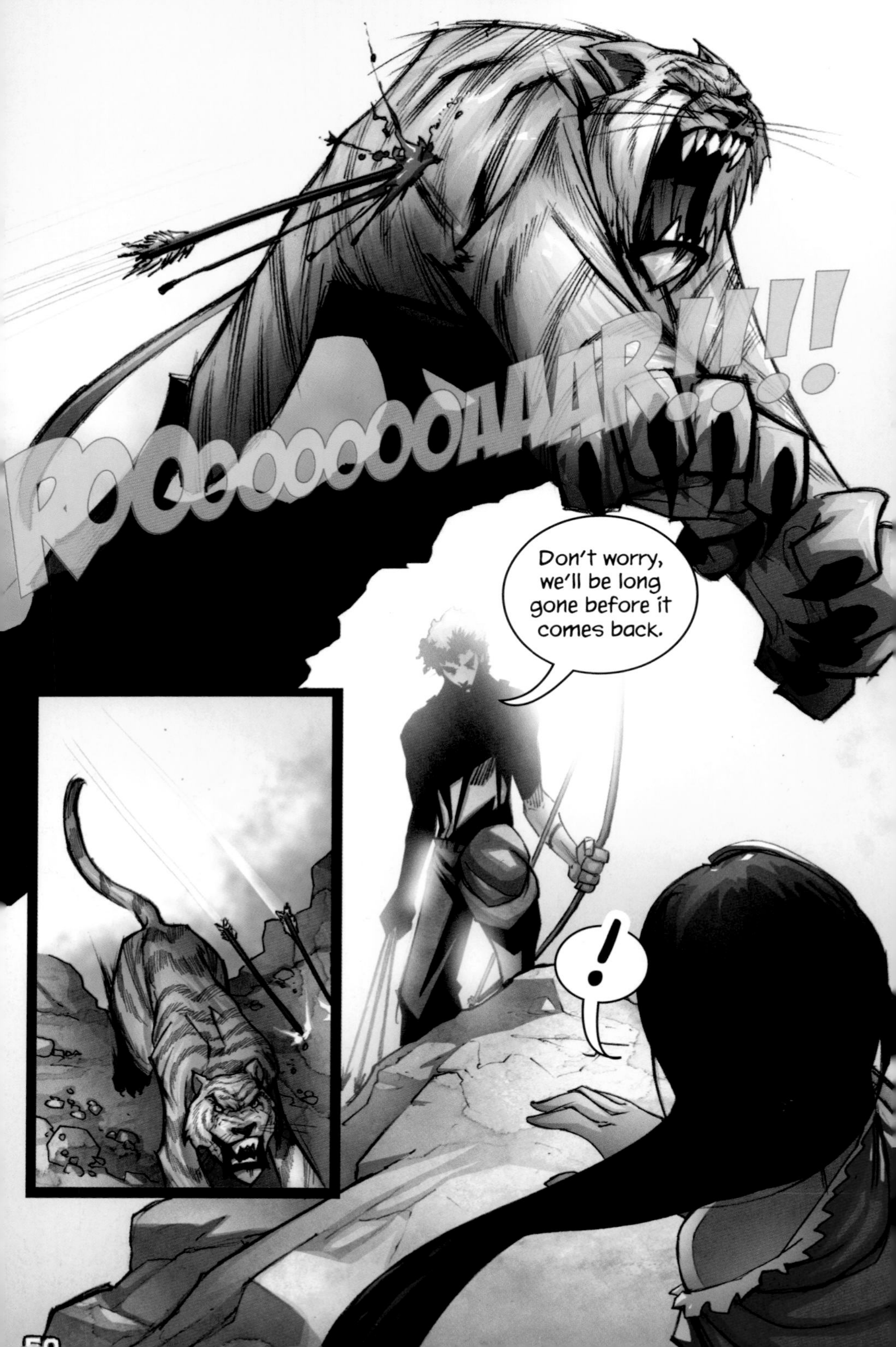
ROOOOOOOOAAAR!!!!!
Don't worry, we'll be long gone before it comes back.
!

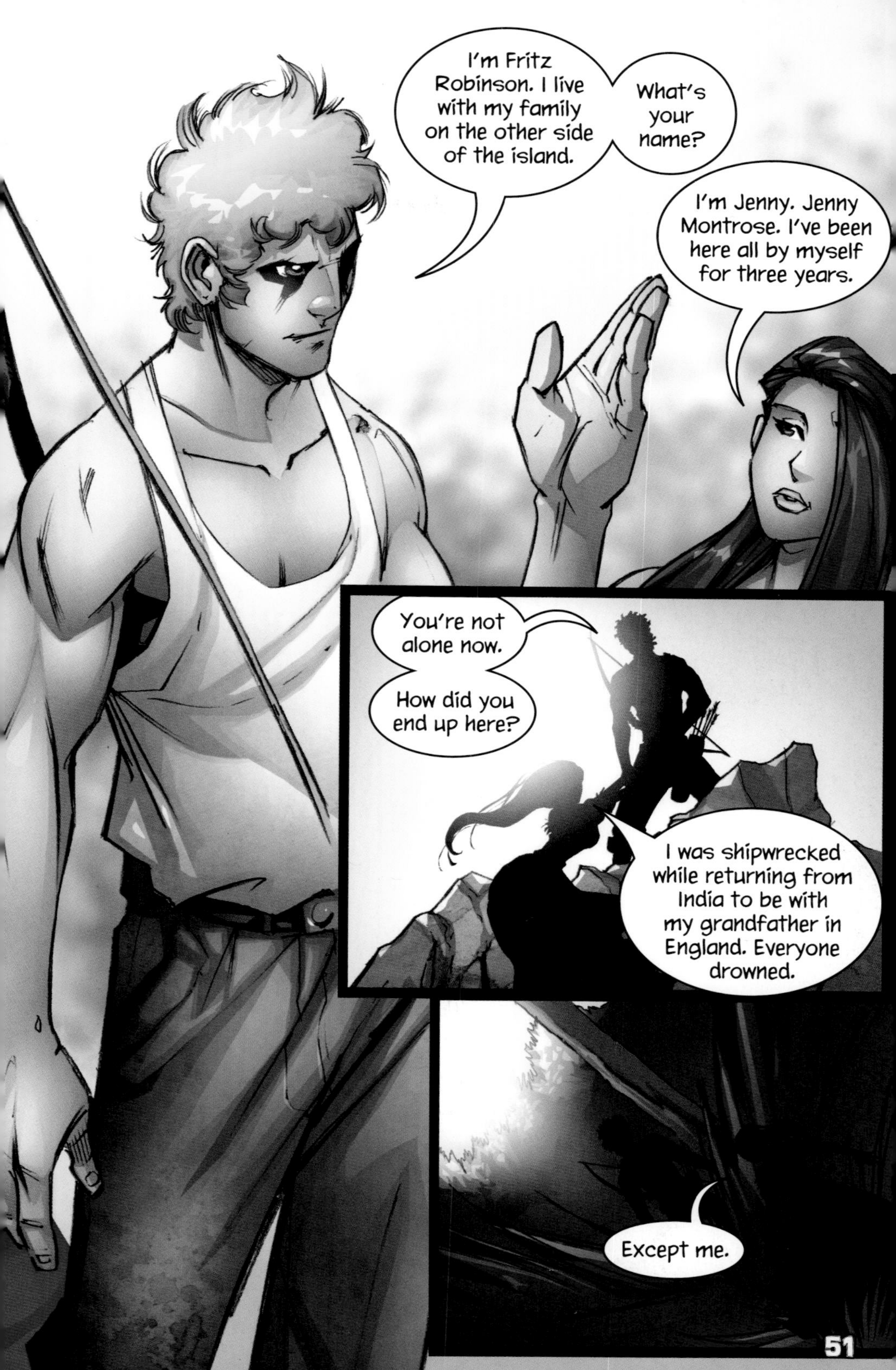
I'm Fritz Robinson. I live with my family on the other side of the island.
What's your name?
I'm Jenny. Jenny Montrose. I've been here all by myself for three years.
You're not alone now.
How did you end up here?
I was shipwrecked while returning from India to be with my grandfather in England. Everyone drowned.
Except me.

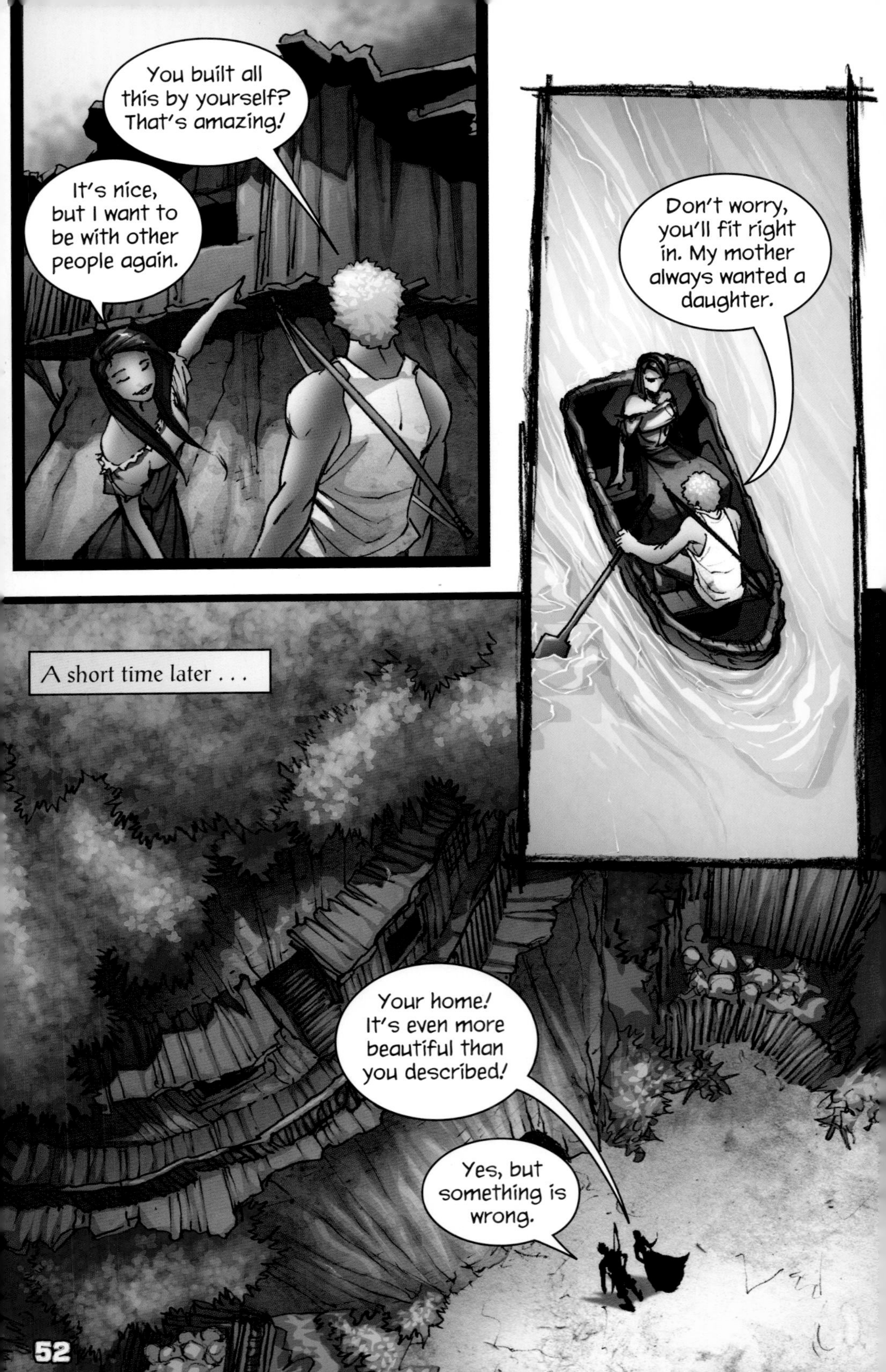
You built all this by yourself? That's amazing!
It's nice, but I want to be with other people again.
Don't worry, you'll fit right in. My mother always wanted a daughter.
A short time later . . .
Your home! It's even more beautiful than you described!
Yes, but something is wrong.

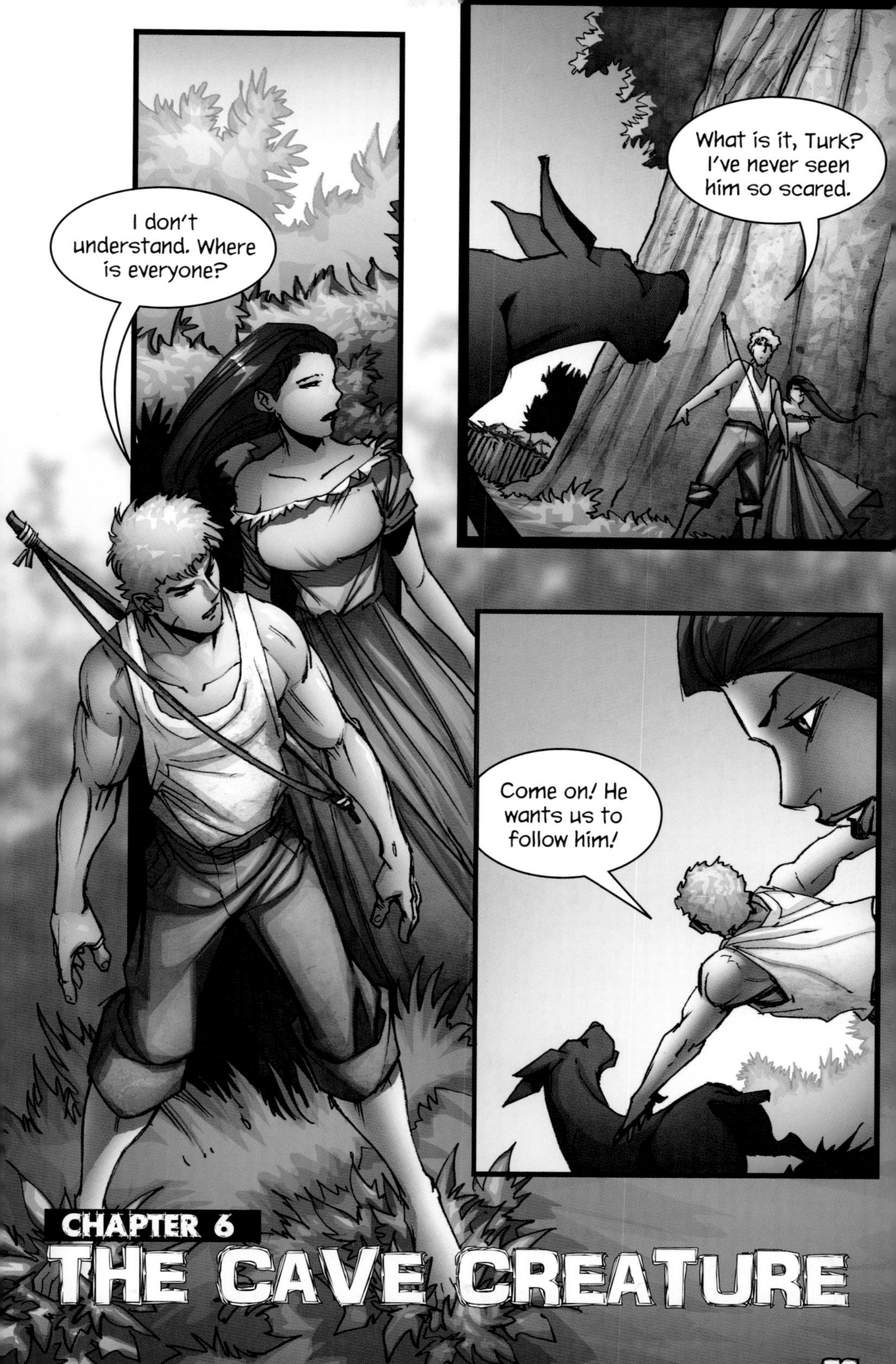
I don't understand. Where is everyone?
What is it, Turk? I've never seen him so scared.
Come on! He wants us to follow him!
CHAPTER 6
THE CAVE CREATURE

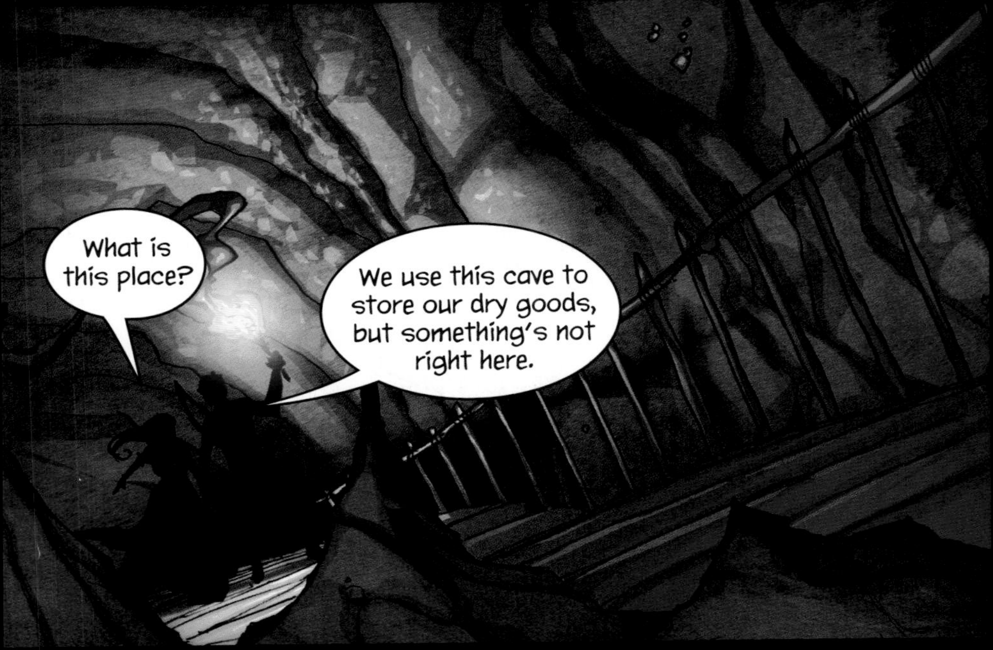
What is this place?
We use this cave to store our dry goods, but something's not right here.

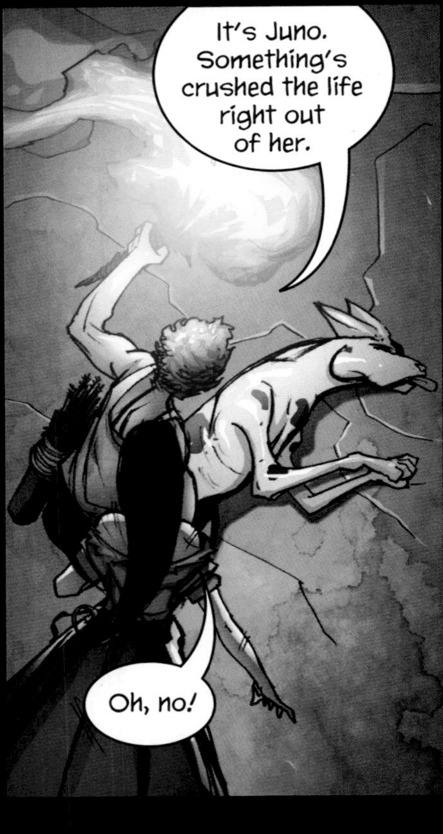
It's Juno. Something's crushed the life right out of her.
Oh, no!

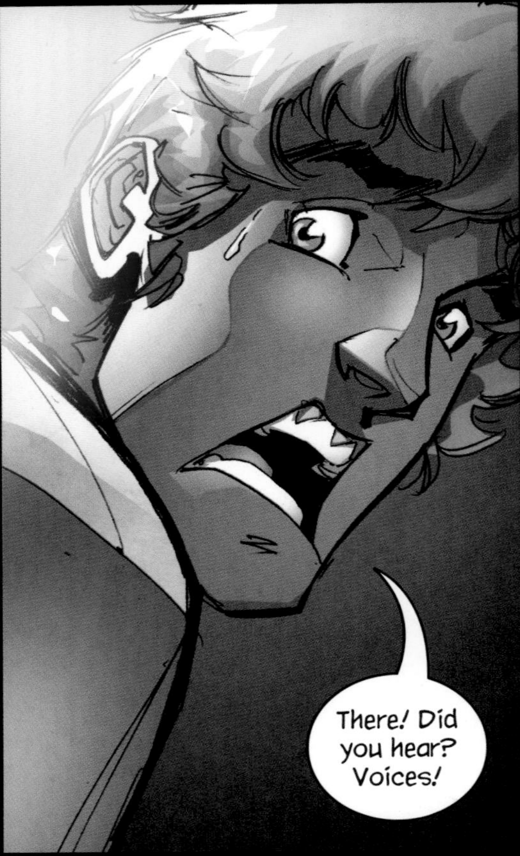
There! Did you hear? Voices!

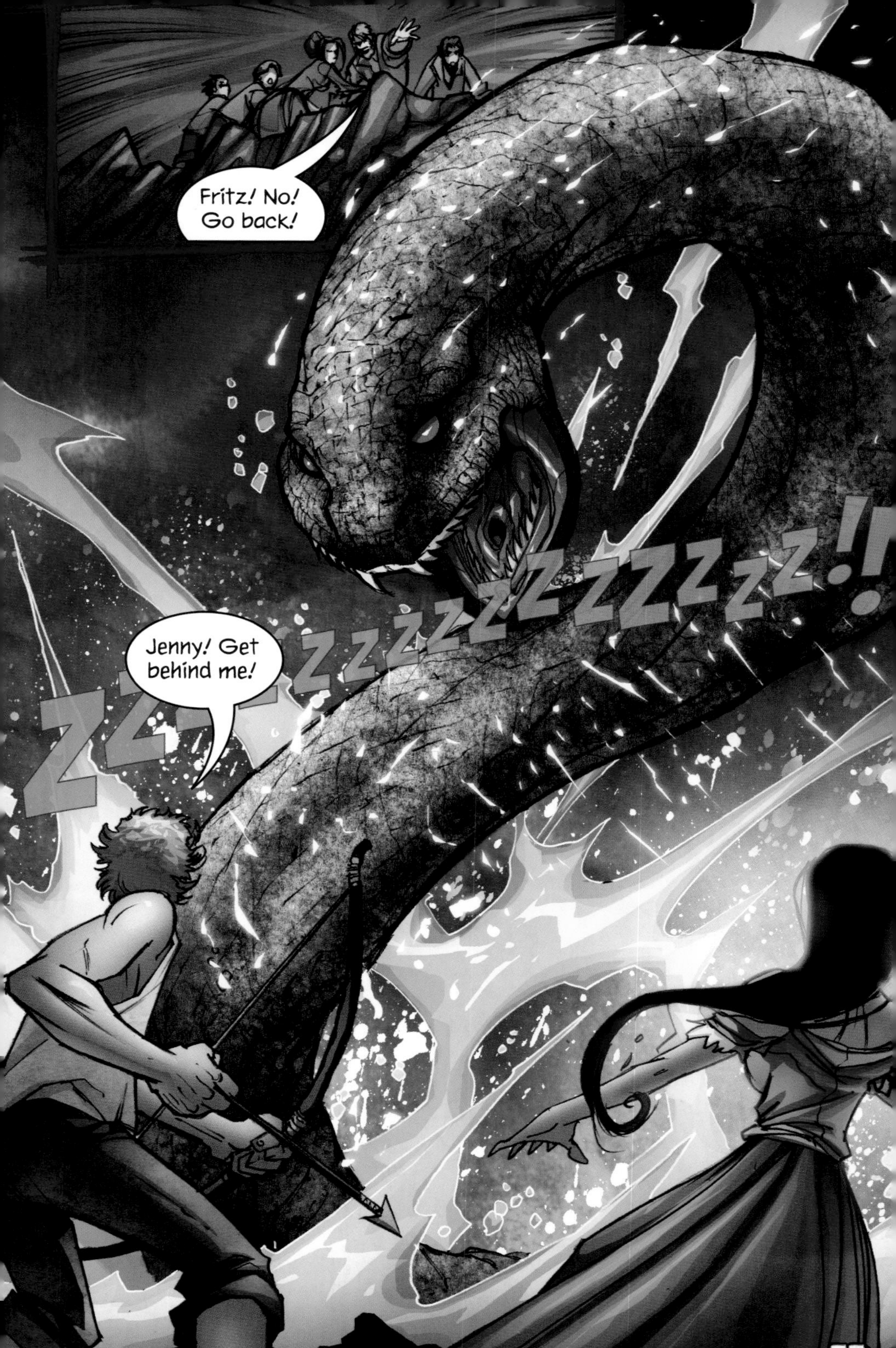
Fritz! No! Go back!
Jenny! Get behind me!
ZZZZZZZZZZZZZZZzz!!

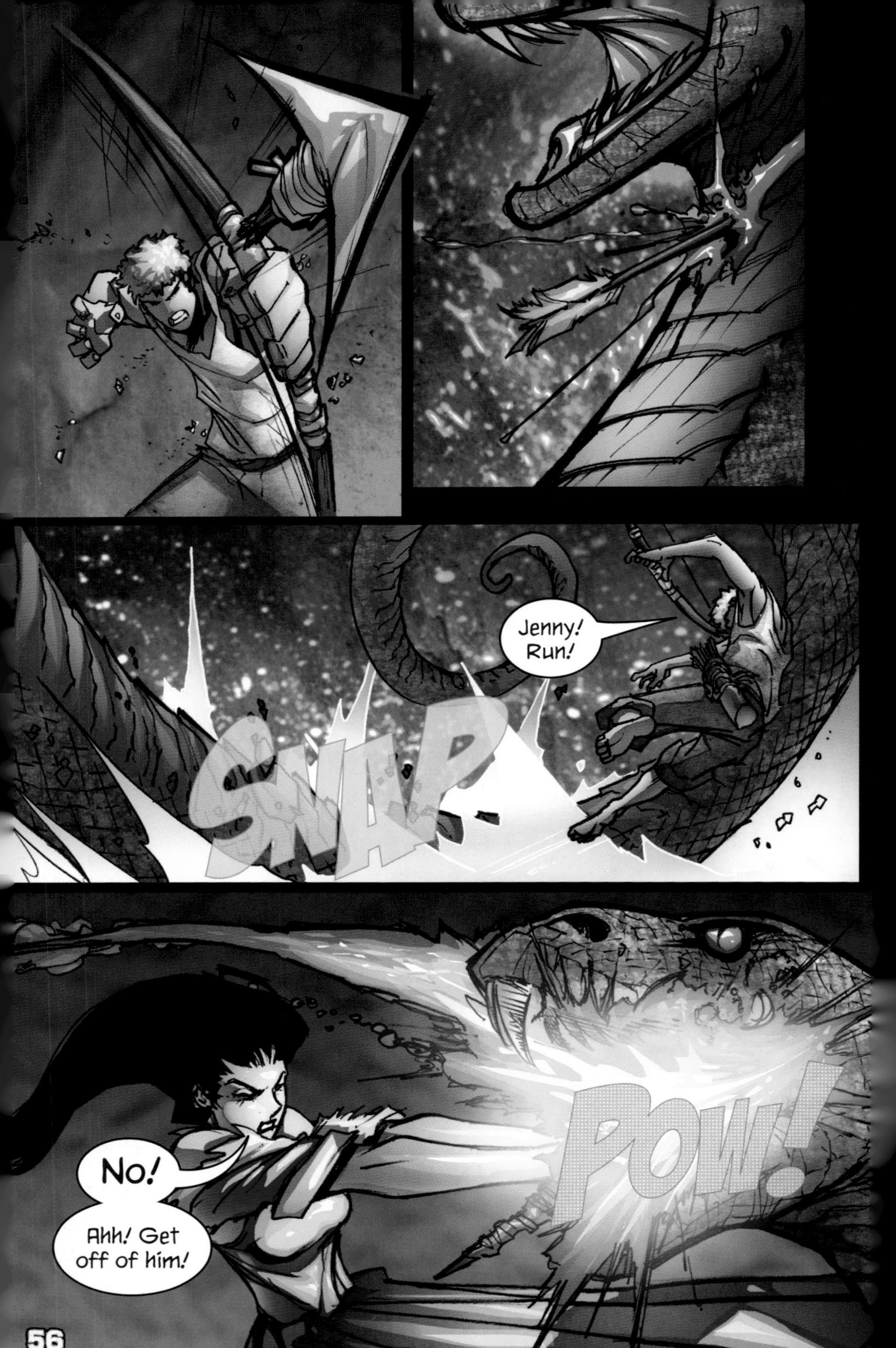
Jenny! Run!
SNAP
POW!
No!
Ahh! Get off of him!

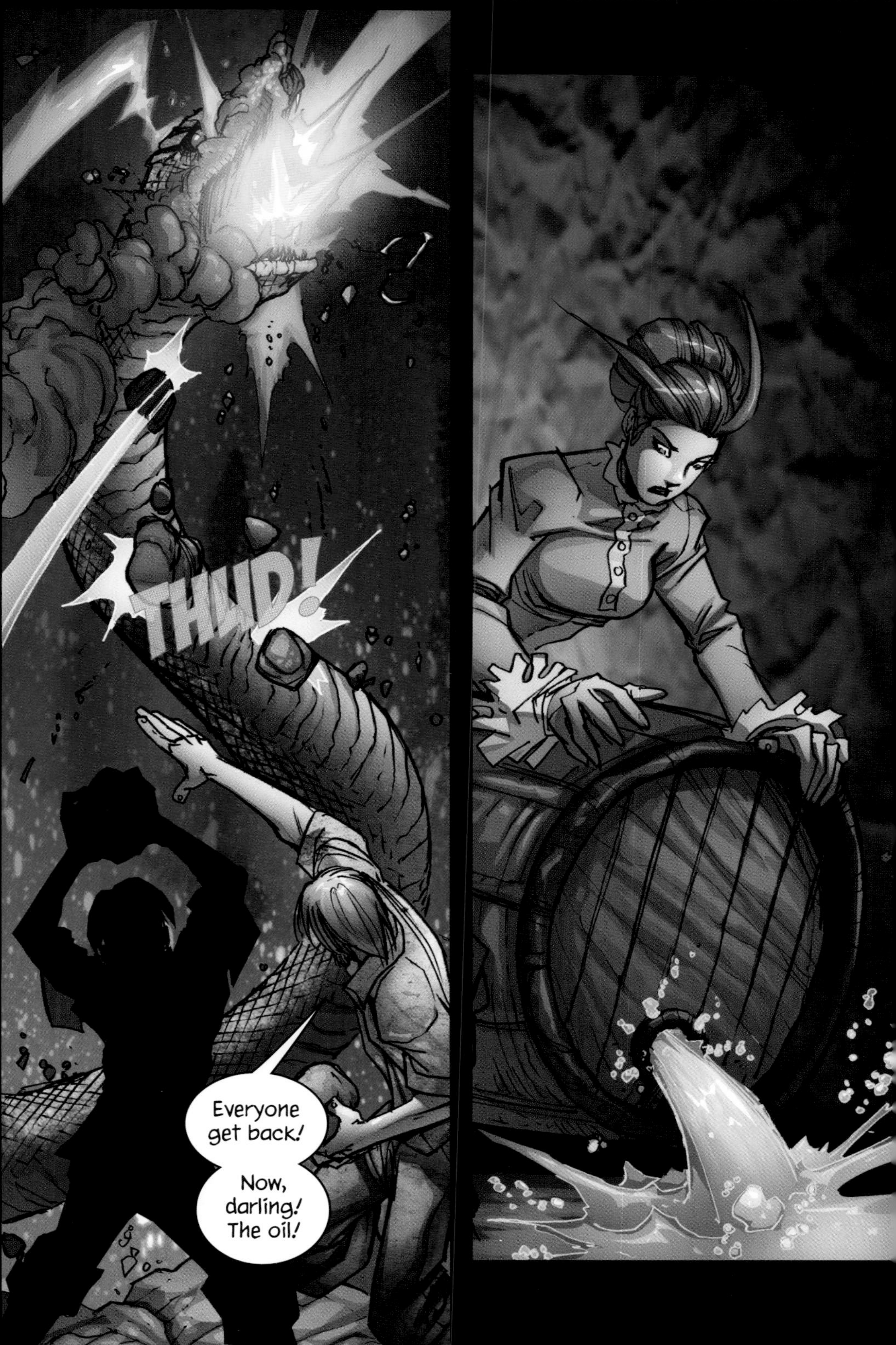
THUD!
Everyone get back!
Now, darling! The oil!

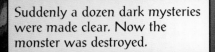
Suddenly a dozen dark mysteries were made clear. Now the monster was destroyed.

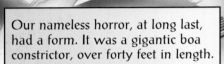
Our nameless horror, at long last, had a form. It was a gigantic boa constrictor, over forty feet in length.

We took Jenny instantly to our hearts. She was braver than any we'd ever known. Now, she had a new family.

And she and Fritz had each other.

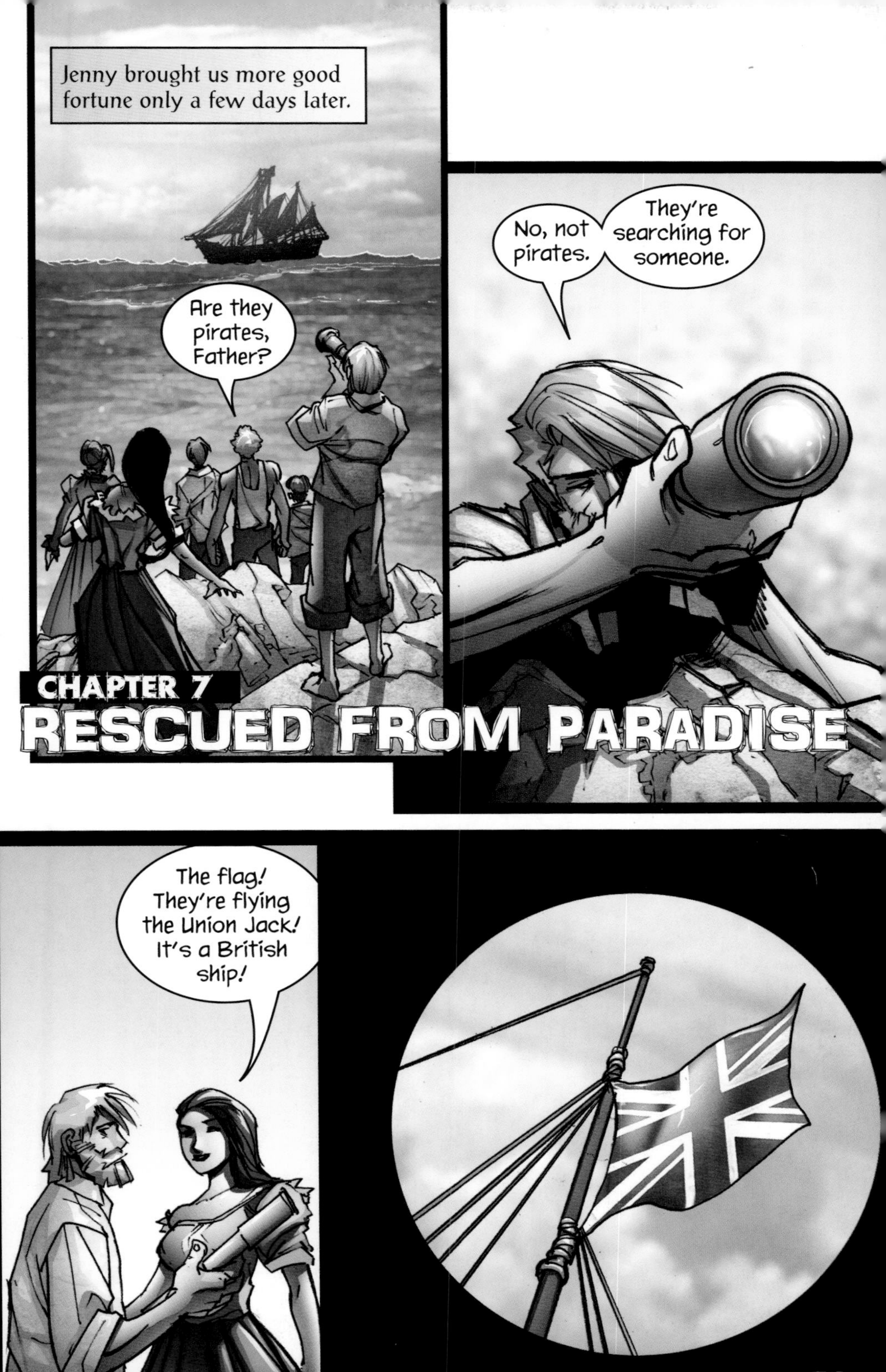
Jenny brought us more good fortune only a few days later.
Are they pirates, Father?
No, not pirates.
They're searching for someone.
CHAPTER 7
RESCUED FROM PARADISE
The flag! They're flying the Union Jack! It's a British ship!

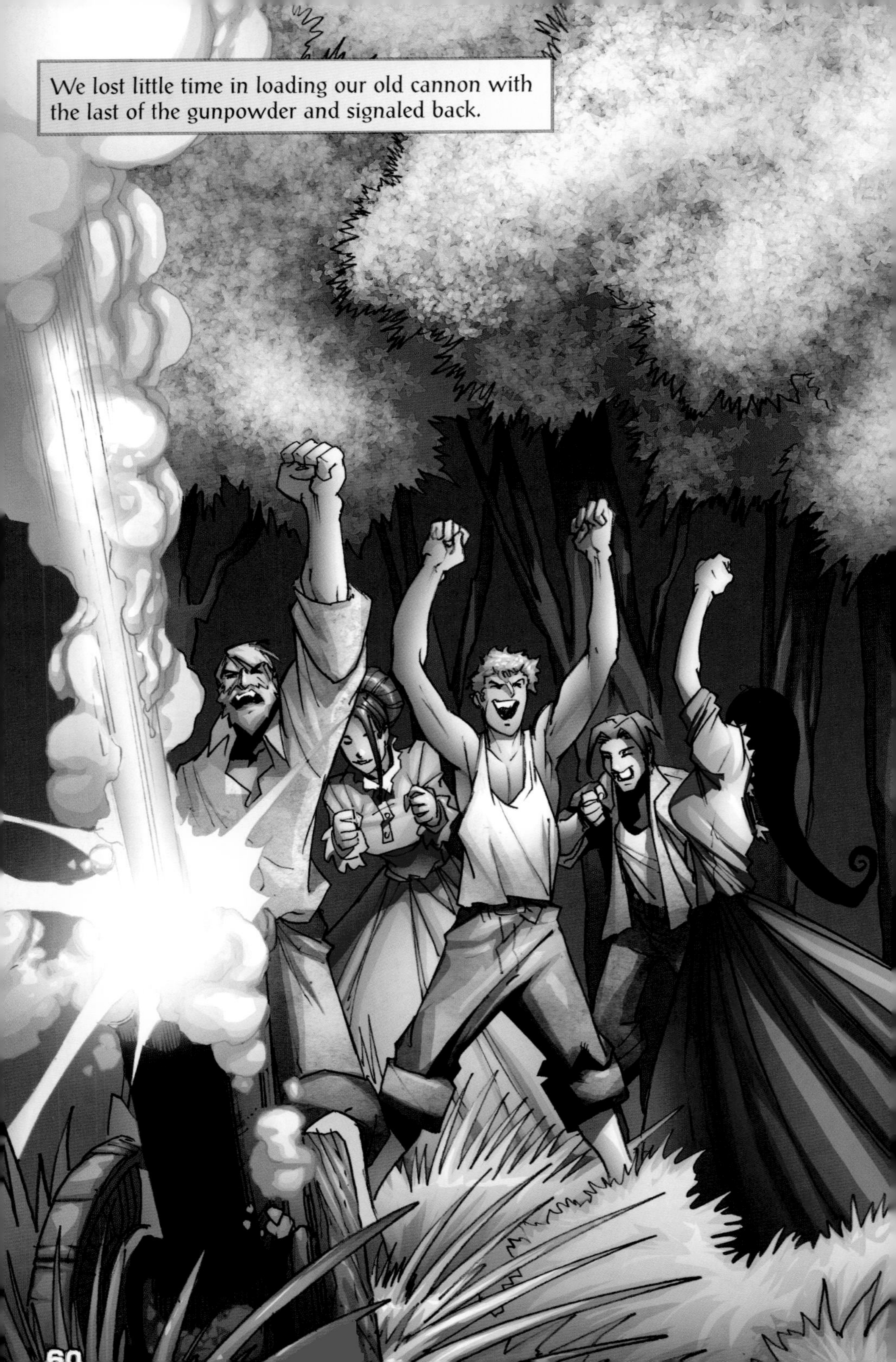
We lost little time in loading our old cannon with the last of the gunpowder and signaled back.

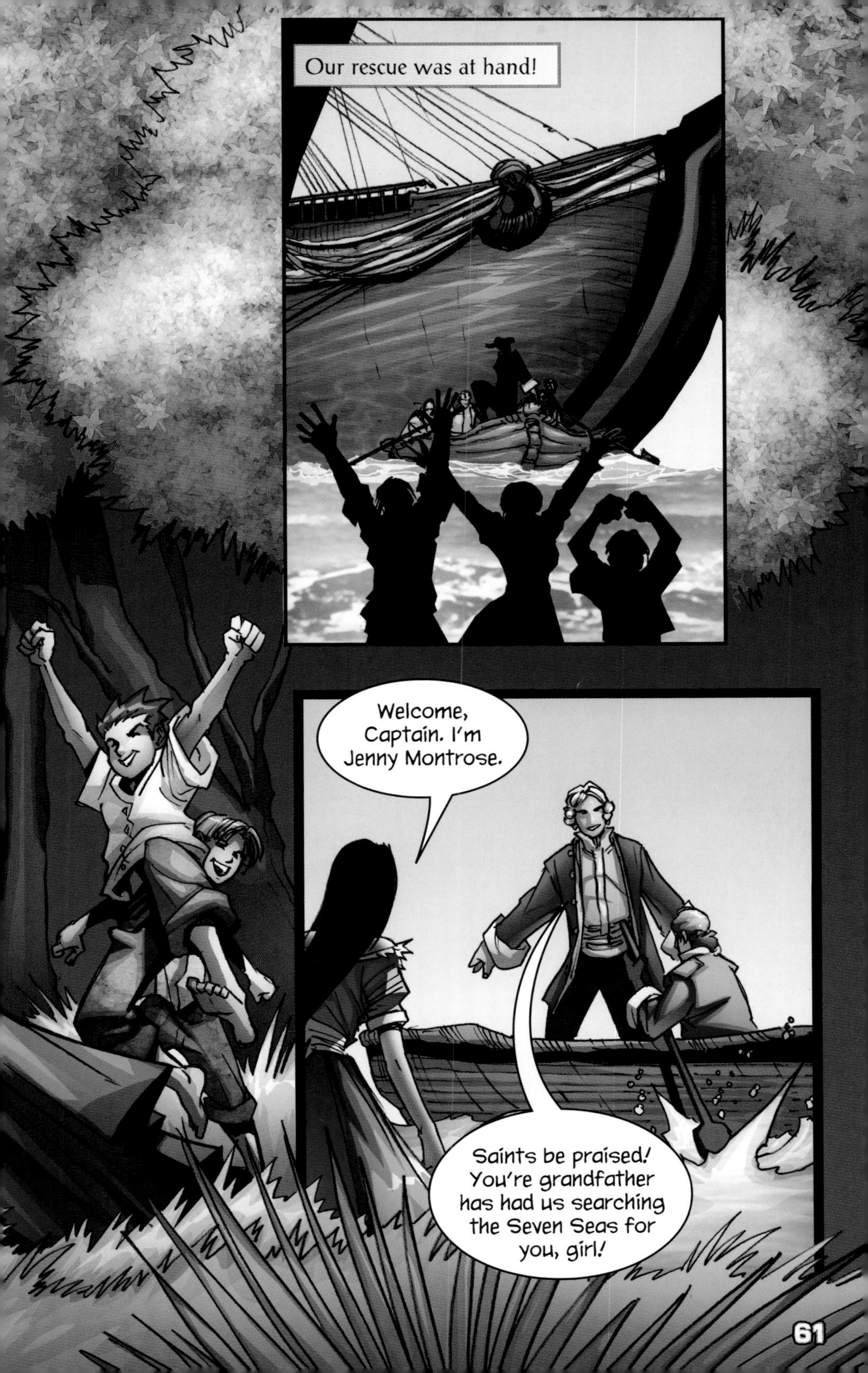
Our rescue was at hand!
Welcome, Captain. I'm Jenny Montrose.
Saints be praised! You're grandfather has had us searching the Seven Seas for you, girl!

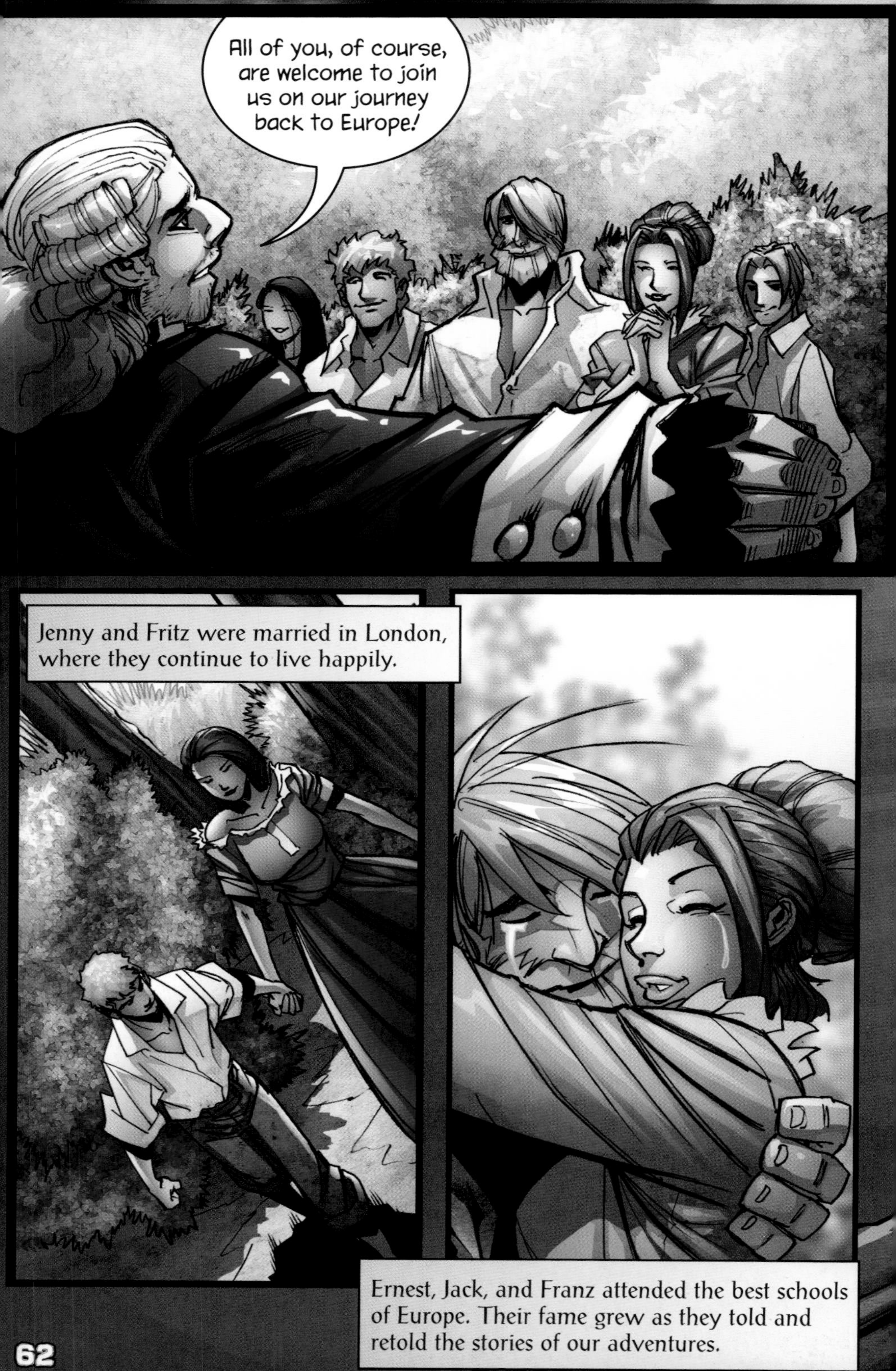
All of you, of course, are welcome to join us on our journey back to Europe!
Jenny and Fritz were married in London, where they continue to live happily.
Ernest, Jack, and Franz attended the best schools of Europe. Their fame grew as they told and retold the stories of our adventures.

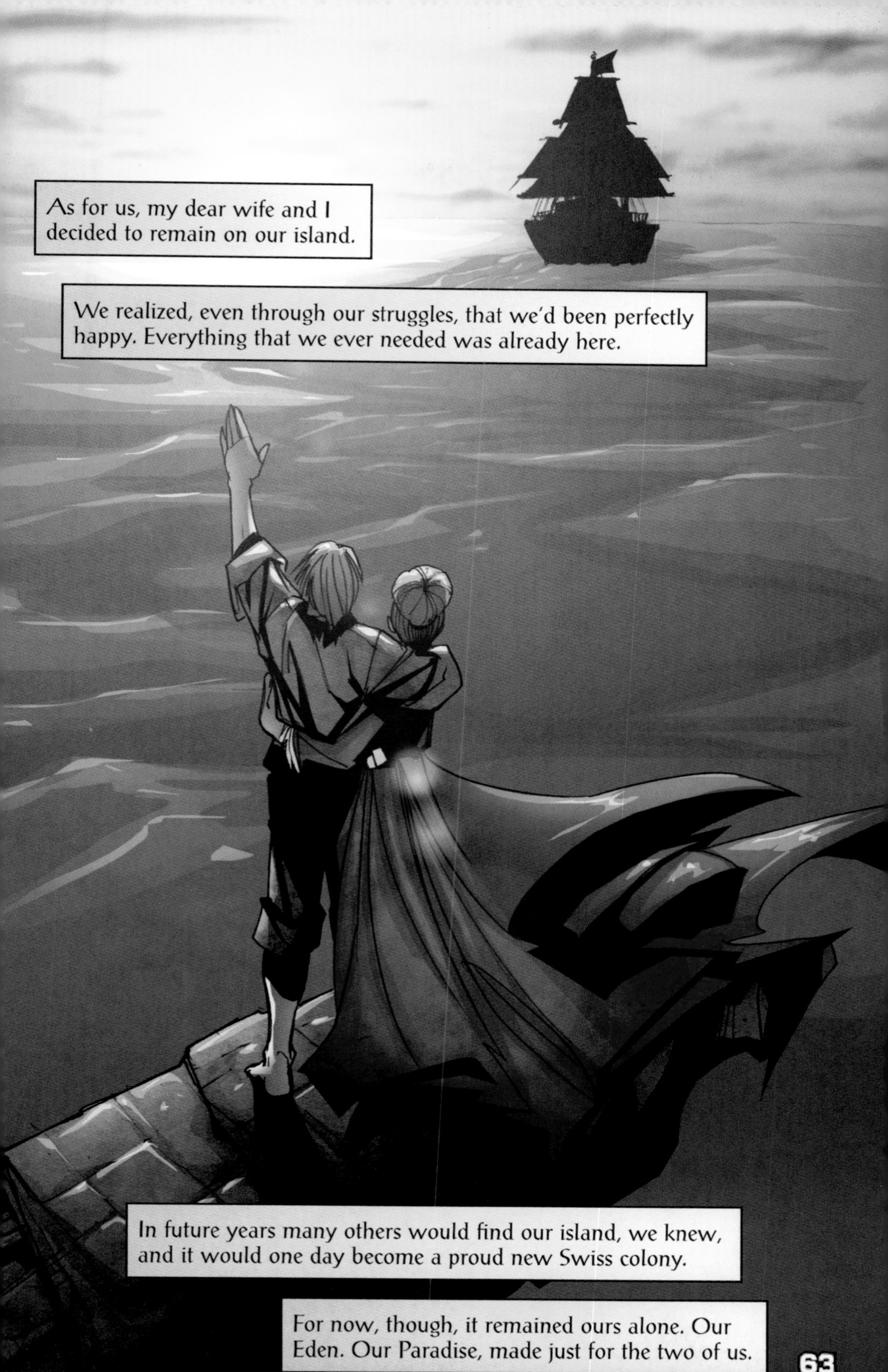
As for us, my dear wife and I decided to remain on our island.
We realized, even through our struggles, that we'd been perfectly happy. Everything that we ever needed was already here.
In future years many others would find our island, we knew, and it would one day become a proud new Swiss colony.
For now, though, it remained ours alone. Our Eden. Our Paradise, made just for the two of us.

ABOUT THE AUTHOR

Born in 1743, Johann David Wyss was a clergyman in Berne, Switzerland. As a military chaplain, Wyss learned four languages, military tactics, and knowledge of the sea-faring life. He used all of this education to write *Swiss Family Robinson* as an adventure story to entertain his four sons. However, the famous book was not published during his own lifetime. One of Wyss' sons, by then a University professor, had the story printed in 1812. It was an instant success. A decade later, the Wyss family commissioned famed French author Madame de Montolieu to expand their book, creating a new ending. *Swiss Family Robinson* has since been published in nearly 200 editions and has never been out of print.

ABOUT THE RETELLING AUTHOR

Since 1986, Martin Powell has been a freelance writer. He has written hundreds of stories, many of which have been published by Disney, Marvel, Tekno Comix, Moonstone Books, and others. In 1989, Powell received an Eisner Award nomination for his graphic novel *Scarlet in Gaslight*. This award is one of the highest comic book honors.

ABOUT THE ILLUSTRATOR

Gerardo Sandoval is a professional comic book illustrator from Mexico. He has worked on many well-known comics including Tomb Raider books from Top Cow Production. He has also worked on designs for posters and card sets.

GLOSSARY

albatross (AL-buh-tross)—a large seabird with webbed feet and long wings that can fly for a long time

horizon (huh-RYE-zuhn)—the line where the sky and the earth or sea seem to meet

looms (LOOMZ)—appears in a sudden or frightening way

magnificent (mag-NIF-i-sent)—very impressive or beautiful

mangroves (MANG-grohvz)—tropical trees

miracles (MEER-uh-kuhlz)—amazing events that cannot be explained by the laws of nature

New Guinea (NOO GIN-ee)—a large island north of Australia that is now called Papua New Guinea

peninsula (puh-NIN-suh-luh)—a piece of land surrounded by water on three sides that sticks out from a larger piece of land

prowling (PROUL-ing)—moving around quietly and secretly. A prowler is someone who is prowling.

savage (SAV-ij)—fierce, dangerous, wild

skulking (SKUHL-king)—hiding and stalking

suspicion (suh-SPISH-uhn)—a thought that is based more on feeling than fact

vanished (VAN-ishd)—disappeared suddenly

MORE ABOUT CASTAWAYS

Many movies, television shows, and books, like *Swiss Family Robinson,* tell stories of people stranded on deserted islands. But could someone really get lost at sea and survive? Below are some interesting facts about becoming a castaway.

Even with more than 6 billion people in the world, finding a place to get stranded isn't that difficult. Thousands of islands have no people at all. In fact, the country of Indonesia has more than 6,000 **uninhabited** (uhn-in-HAB-uh-tid) islands.

The largest uninhabited island in the world isn't small at all. Devon Island in Canada is an impressive 21,231 square miles (55,000 square kilometers). That's nearly as big as the state of West Virginia!

Finding a place to get lost is easy, but how long could a human survive without food, water, or TV? Surprisingly, humans can last nearly a month without any food at all. In fact, magician David Blaine lasted an incredible 44 days without eating in 2003. Finding water is much more important. Experts say that more than three days without water could be deadly. And life without TV? Well, it might be painful, but it won't kill you.

If you are stranded on a deserted island, look for coconuts. These nuts are an excellent source of both food and liquid. The husks can be used to make rope, and coconut oil can help repel pesky insects such as mosquitoes.

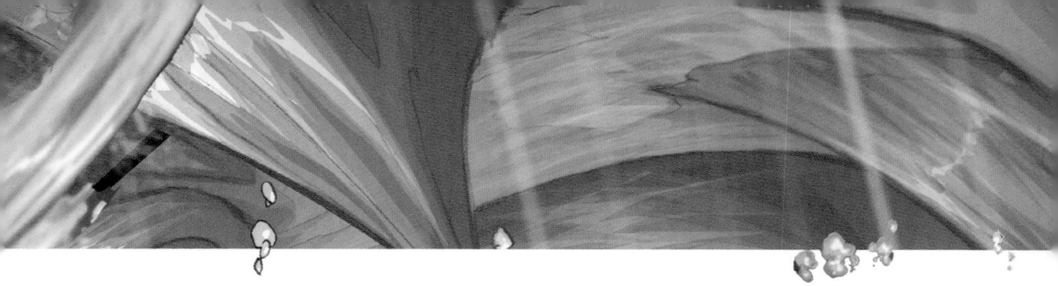

So, surviving on a deserted island is possible (at least for a while), but has anyone ever done it? Many people have lasted a few days after a shipwreck or a plane crash, but only a few can be called real-life castaways.

Perhaps the most famous castaway was a Scottish sailor named Alexander Selkirk. In September 1704, Selkirk was left stranded on a small island off the coast of Chile. With only a few tools, a musket, and a Bible, Selkirk survived alone for the next four years and four months. After he was rescued in February 1709, Selkirk wrote a book about his experience. A few years later, author Daniel Defoe turned Selkirk's story into a famous fiction novel called *Robinson Crusoe.* This book has inspired many other adventure stories, including *Swiss Family Robinson.*

Another famous castaway, Tom Neale, wasn't stranded on a deserted island—he chose to live there! In 1952, Neale settled on a small island in the Pacific Ocean called Suwarrow. With only a few supplies, he lived by himself on the island for 15 of the next 25 years. He grew small gardens, raised chickens, caught fish, and ate coconuts. Shortly after his death in 1977, the island was declared a National Heritage Park. A small memorial on the island reads, "Tom Neale lived his dream on this island."

DISCUSSION QUESTIONS

1. The deserted island in *Swiss Family Robinson* is filled with thousands of different types of plants and animals. Do you think all of these animals could actually live together? Why or why not?

2. Throughout the story, the family has to work together to survive on the deserted island. Which family member do you think helps out the most? Explain your answer using examples from the story.

3. At the end of the story, Mr Robinson and Mrs. Robinson decide to stay on the island. Why do you think they made this decision? Would you have stayed on the island or returned home? Explain your answers.

WRITING PROMPTS

1. Make a list of five things you would want to have on a deserted island. Would you want matches, a fishing pole, or maybe your favorite book? When your list is completed, explain why you chose each item.

2. How would you get off of a deserted island? Remember, you can only use items found on the island. Explain your plan.

3. Mr. Robinson and Mrs. Robinson chose to stay on the island instead of returning. If you could choose to live anywhere in the world, where would you live? Explain why you would live there and what your life would be like.

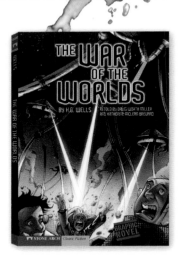

OTHER BOOKS

THE WAR OF THE WORLDS
BY H.G. WELLS
RETOLD BY DAVIS WORTH MILLER AND KATHERINE MCLEAN BREVARD
GRAPHIC NOVEL
STONE ARCH Classic Fiction

The War of the Worlds

In the late 19th century, a cylinder crashes down near London. When George investigates, a Martian activates an evil machine and begins destroying everything in its path! George must find a way to survive a War of the Worlds.

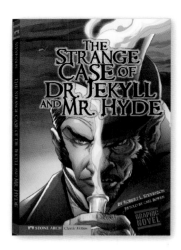

THE STRANGE CASE OF DR. JEKYLL AND MR. HYDE
BY ROBERT L. STEVENSON
RETOLD BY CARL BOWEN
GRAPHIC NOVEL
STONE ARCH Classic Fiction

The Strange Case of Dr. Jekyll and Mr. Hyde

Scientist Dr. Henry Jekyll believes every human has two minds: one good and one evil. He develops a potion to separate them from each other. Soon, his evil mind takes over, and Dr. Jekyll becomes a hideous fiend known as Mr. Hyde.

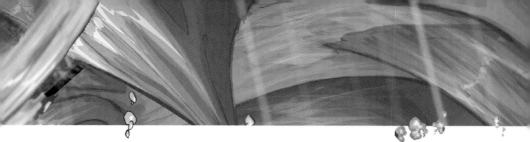

The HOUND of the BASKERVILLES
by Sir Arthur Conan Doyle
retold by Martin Powell
GRAPHIC NOVEL
STONE ARCH Classic Fiction

The Hound of the Baskervilles

Late one night, Sir Charles Baskerville is attacked outside his castle in Dartmoor, England. Could it be the Hound of the Baskervilles, a legendary creature that haunts the nearby moor? Sherlock Holmes, the world's greatest detective, is on the case.

Jonathan Swift
GRAPHIC NOVEL
Jonathan Swift's
GULLIVER'S TRAVELS
STONE ARCH Classic Fiction

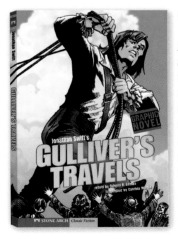

Gulliver's Travels

Lemuel Gulliver always dreamed of sailing across the seas, but he never could have imagined the places his travels would take him. On the island of Lilliput, he is captured by tiny creatures no more than six inches tall. In the country of Blefuscu, he is nearly squashed by an army of giants. His adventures could be the greatest tales ever told, if he survives long enough to tell them.

INTERNET SITES

Do you want to know more about subjects related to this book? Or are you interested in learning about other topics? Then check out FactHound, a fun, easy way to find Internet sites.

Our investigative staff has already sniffed out great sites for you!

Here's how to use FactHound:

1. Visit www.facthound.com

2. Select your grade level.

3. To learn more about subjects related to this book, type in the book's ISBN number: **9781434207562**.

4. Click the **Fetch It** button.

FactHound will fetch the best Internet sites for you!